"*The End*, a riotous, sex-stuffed novel by Torres, which takes Technicolor pleasure in detailing the deaths of five incorrigible old beach bums of the Bossa Nova generation. . . . Her five men, whom she kills off in reverse chronology, are 'united by male allegiance, women, and the beach, in that order'. . . . With America undergoing a mass reckoning with male sexuality, a novel like this feels both taboo and gleeful, a guilty kind of reprieve."

HERMIONE HOBY, *THE NEW YORKER*

"The intense but tenuous bonds of male friendship give shape and structure to this energetic, impressive debut from acclaimed Brazilian actress Torres. Set against the vivid backdrop of Copacabana, the episodic novel follows five contentious and devoted friends—Ciro, Silvio, Neto, Alvaro, and Ribeiro—from the hedonistic nights of their youth to the humbling days of old age. Beginning with the violent death of Alvaro, the group's last surviving member, the story meticulously works its way back through the complicated lives of each friend, culminating with the operatic death of Ciro, who retains a spark of youth until his last moments. Torres paints a sharp, intimate portrait of ... ality and psychology (inclu ... ninating the friends' profou ... decadent Silvio and the me ... ing the believability

of their connection. As assured as the characterizations of the central characters are the investigations of the men and women who surround them, the wives who abide their exploits and the priests who speak at their funerals. The narration and momentum remain lively and sharp throughout."

PUBLISHERS WEEKLY, STARRED REVIEW

"Set in Rio de Janeiro, this fine literary debut from one of Brazil's most distinguished actors tells the stories of five men as they approach their inevitable (and in some cases premature) ends. By turns tragic and hilarious, the novel is about friendship, betrayal and excess, and about male fury against the ravages of old age."

ÁNGEL GURRÍA-QUINTANA, *FINANCIAL TIMES*

"*The End* is the perfect summer release. Torres creates an aging, male Carioca friend group that is a mess of cynicism, nostalgia, frustration, and a seemingly unending appetite for sex. This book is raunchy, sophisticated, and so wonderfully Brazilian. I devoured this book in one sitting. Parabens Fernanda!!!"

DANIELA ROGER, BOOKS & BOOKS (CORAL GABLES, FL)

"The year of 2013 would have been worth it for Fernanda Torres' novel alone. How beautiful it is to see an authentic literary talent emerge so clearly. . . . In her debut *The End*, she goes beyond just being a good writer. Her tone is so well crafted."

CAETANO VELOSO

"You think you see *The End* coming—or the ending coming— but Fernanda Torres has other plans for you on this journey. Torres presents five friends—fairly flawed, tragic clowns— and their views on life and those around them as they try to navigate their lives and deaths. This novel is a funny, smart, well conceived, and perfectly executed playful look at mortality."

"Famed actress Fernanda Torres' debut novel, *The End*, is a brutally unflinching look at the lifelong friendships of five aging male friends and the women in their lives. . . . [Torres has an] agile hand at establishing voice, pacing, and tone. Hers is strong, economical prose. . . . The machismo of each character is impressively rendered. . . . *The End* is vivid and irascible as it confronts the reality of aging, regrets, and death."

"Torres' darkly humorous first novel conjures a unique time in Brazilian history through a clever narrative conceit and vividly portrayed characters."

"Torres' writing [has] flair and wit . . . [an] unforgiving portrait of men at their worst."

GLORY AND ITS LITANY OF HORRORS

ALSO BY FERNANDA TORRES

The End

FERNANDA TORRES

GLORY AND ITS LITANY OF HORRORS

A NOVEL

**TRANSLATED FROM THE PORTUGUESE
BY ERIC M. B. BECKER**

RESTLESS BOOKS
BROOKLYN, NEW YORK

First published in Portuguese as *A glória e seu cortejo de horrores*
by Companhia das Letras Ltda. in 2017.

First Restless Books paperback edition July 2019

Paperback ISBN: 9781632061126
Library of Congress Control Number: 2019933970

Cover design by Na Kim
Set in Garibaldi by Tetragon, London

Printed in Canada

1 3 5 7 9 10 8 6 4 2

Restless Books, Inc.
232 3rd Street, Suite A101
Brooklyn, NY 11215

www.restlessbooks.org
publisher@restlessbooks.org

This project is supported in part by an award from
the National Endowment for the Arts.

This book is made possible by the New York State Council on the Arts with the
support of Governor Andrew M. Cuomo and the New York State Legislature.

Obra publicada com o apoio do Ministério da Cultura do Brasil |
Fundação Biblioteca Nacional.
This work is published with the support of the Ministry of
Culture of Bazil | Fundação Biblioteca Nacional.

For Arlette and Fernanda
to whom I owe my life
the wings
and the title of this book

GLORY AND ITS LITANY OF HORRORS

PART I

Pillicock sat on Pillicock-hill:
Halloo, halloo, loo, loo!

SHAKESPEARE,
KING LEAR, ACT 3, SC. 4

ONE MOMENT was all it took—*Blow, winds*, I howled amid the storm, despite the hoarseness that had dogged me since opening night; the cast shook their metal thunder sheets, the inane idea of the genius director with ambitions of outshining even Shakespeare. The tense rehearsals, the disaster that is Portuguese, employing three times as many words as English to say the exact same thing, my head spinning from one scene to another, and another, and another, BAM. Any illusion that things were somehow improving went down the drain the day the reinventor of the wheel handed strips of sheet metal to all the actors and ordered the idiots to shake the damn things with the fury of wild beasts. A laughingstock, thanks to the fact that yours truly, in addition to playing the lead role, was the one paying all those people to be there: the one behind the production who'd had the brilliant idea to go after corporate charitable contributions to achieve his dream of being something more than a mediocre actor of the tropics.

> *Blow, winds, and crack your cheeks! rage! blow!*
> *You cataracts and hurricanoes, spout*
> *Till you have drench'd our steeples, drown'd the cocks!*

5

In the two months leading up to the premiere, the voice coach, a cross between a shaman and a doctor honoris causa, had me repeat the storm soliloquy on all fours atop her rug in some decrepit office tower in Copacabana. I did as she instructed, there on all fours, on the rug, trusting her theory that this was the only way I would reach the depths of the King's humiliation. Brazil lacks any sort of royal sentiment: we're a bunch of plebes, we jeer our King Joãos and our Prince Pedros, the republic we founded was a half-assed job. Laurence Olivier would never have been made to get down on all fours, but there I was, on all fours, in a cubicle in Copacabana. I knew all about humiliation; what I lacked was the dignity to wear a crown, none of us have it. I was certain of that each time I left the cramped room in the office tower on Rua Figueiredo Magalhães, somewhere between depressed and exhausted, on my way to yet another grueling day of rehearsals. At the time, I still clung to hope. The illusion of glory. Everything began to fall apart the day the asshole director handed the cast their metal thunderbolts and told the beasts to wag the damn things. *Stein*, I said (the visionary's name was Stein), *no one's going to hear a word with all that going on*. He sneered and told me it wasn't the words that mattered, only the deconstruction of the text and some nonsense about the theater of images. *Go direct a puppet show*, I thought, *you could send for those giant dolls they march through the streets at Carnaval*. I was about to explode, but fear of losing the director a month before the premiere convinced me to hold my horses.

Center stage, I repeated the verses with my paws on the ground, a king without a kingdom, Lear incarnate. In my distress, my mind turned to exorcism, black magic, I considered suicide and even murder. Stein's, of course. These homicidal thoughts are what kept me going right up through the final dress. The satisfaction of all that rage. In the place of Goneril and Regan, the callous daughters of the monarch without a throne, all I saw was Stein; I unleashed my hate upon him and I felt better, even too much better. That ingrate hadn't directed a production in more than ten years. I'd rescued him from his farm in Corrêas, the hideaway where the great promise of eighties theater had taken refuge after declaring humanity incapable of understanding his sublime creativity.

> *And thou, all-shaking thunder,*
> *Smite flat the thick rotundity o' the world!*
> *Crack nature's moulds, all germains spill at once,*
> *That make ingrateful man!*

This loathing for the director was only one of my problems. The scenographer and the costume designer, two old married queens who only worked together, made the nightmare complete. The first dreamed up a medieval castle wall that took a forest's worth of the finest wood. The giant logs were so heavy that I was forced to hire an engineer to reinforce the beams beneath the stage. *Stage*—it was a theater in the middle of a shopping center, a transvestite England. *That's the set*, I repeated, but the boy wonder wanted "truth." *Easy to say when someone else is footing the bill*, I bristled, and he stormed off, as though I were some stingy philistine who lacked the sensibility

7

to drink from the font of his inspiration. The castle moat took up three rows in front of the stage, cutting into the profits of those earning a percentage. The children's show on Saturdays and Sundays meant we had to tear down the circus twice a week, weighing down the payroll with three more jugheads. In addition to these imbeciles, four more amateurs took turns as stagehands. Stein demanded more truth and dreamed up two banquets found nowhere in the original. We consumed ten rotisserie chickens per rehearsal, not to mention the overpriced fruit, bread, and vegetables bought at the corner market, only to rot mercilessly in the dressing room. The smell was awful. In the scenes where Lear is expelled from his house by his daughters, a gate—operated by two chains—would slam shut. We spent a week rigging up the contraption. To hell with poetry, Stein wanted action. When we came to the war scene, though I tried my best to convince him otherwise, nothing could dissuade the moron from setting fire to the parapets along the castle walls, covered entirely in Styrofoam painted to look like stone. I hired a fireman to be on standby. Stein demanded that, after dying, Cordelia enter nude in her father's arms. The actress was a cute little thing, and Stein tried everything he could think of to nail her, without success. She had a head on her, that girl. The Sunday before the premiere, the fireman gave in to his hormones and copped a feel of the girl's breasts. I canned the perv. His replacement only snuck a peek every now and then, and I asked the girl to grin and bear it. After watching a Russian film production of *Lear*, Stein decided to set the whole thing in the Stone Age. The costume designer had multiple orgasms at the idea and presented us all with an entire collection of sheepskins—he'd wanted bear but settled for sheep. We sweat like pigs, dragging the furry capes around in the summer heat. The curtain rose soon after Carnaval, the air-conditioning was useless, and because they only turned it on when there was a show—*mustn't be wasteful, Horacio, mustn't be wasteful*—two actors ended up in the hospital, further compromising the lead-up to opening night.

The old hag who was lead critic at Rio's major daily consummated the tragedy. A Shakespeare scholar, the iron lady made her living watching the lowest kind of musicals on stages across Brazil. Though she could forgive cheap comedies, a cruel hostility befell those, like me, who made an effort to take on the canon. She opened her review with my epitaph and closed it decrying public arts funding for allowing such an unfortunate production to see the light of day. A pall fell over the cast. We still had six months to go and a sponsorship contract stipulating a run in São Paulo. The catastrophe in Rio closed to an empty house, we crammed the castle into four moving trucks, and set off for the second leg of our tour.

São Paulo. I finally succumbed in São Paulo.

The engineering firm that had sponsored the run decided to celebrate its fiftieth anniversary by inviting its employees to the premiere. In the lobby, before the show, they served a four-cheese pasta with mushrooms, along with some cheap domestic red. Having spent all day hard at work, the guests stuffed themselves with food and alcohol. The curtain was barely up before the first snores echoed across the theater.

Since the slightest dramatic pause amplified this Symphony of Morpheus, we began to avoid them as best as we could. We sped through our speaking parts; the faster we rushed through the text, the longer the play dragged on. It was like torture: slow, endless, unbearable. When the lights came up, we patiently waited for half the audience to wake the other so they could reward us for our efforts with yawns and half-hearted applause.

The leading morning newspaper delivered the flogging. A critic ought to have the decency not to show up at the theater on sponsor night, but this one did not. None of them do.

Compared to the São Paulo review, the one that ran in Rio was practically a coronation. On the bottom of page four of the entertainment section, wedged between the comics and the horoscopes, a tiny black-and-white photo of me on all fours embellished the headline: A MIDSUMMER NIGHTMARE. The wise guy began his analysis by listing the actors suffering from delusions of grandeur. I lacked the gravitas for the role of Lear, he decreed, concluding that even Romeo would be a better fit. Regretting I'd not opted for *Macbeth*, I began to hatch a plan to blow up the newsroom with the wretch inside. He was twenty-eight years old, the damn upstart, and suffered from the same inferiority complex as all the other journalists working at that newspaper. In barely five paragraphs, he tore everything apart: cast, director, lighting, scenery, costumes; only the Fool, played by Arlindo Correia, escaped the fiasco unscathed. An old theater actor who, like the rest of us, had earned his living on TV, Arlindo had been part of historic productions: he'd worked with Kusnet, Ziembinski, and had belonged to the Teatro de

Arena chorus. He shined from the very first reading, he had a knack for switching between irony and tragedy at just the right moment. During rehearsals, I tried to hide the envy of knowing he would come off better than I would—and without the weight of carrying the entire production on his shoulders. I kept my poker face as best I could, until I read the naked truth in that newspaper fancying itself the *New York Times*. I began to avoid him, I even stopped greeting him. I would arrive at the theater early, mutter an inaudible *Hello*, and slip into the dressing room practically unnoticed. My only comfort, if you can call it that, was listening to Lineu Castro swear up and down as he arranged his white beard.

Lineu was a marvelous actor, neurotic but marvelous. He had terrible sexual hangups, he'd been a virgin until the age of twenty-eight and must have screwed a woman all of two times in his entire life. One of those times, a child was conceived. Lineu was a hypochondriac and took only occasional showers. No one wanted to share a dressing room with him. We ended up together there in front of the mirror, I listened as he went on and on about how miserable life was with his ugly wife and loser kid. Misfortune had gifted him with a sensibility that was rare in an actor. It wasn't vanity that moved him but a deep understanding of human pettiness. That's what led us to cast him in the role of Gloucester, a father betrayed by his bastard son, the villain Edmund, who plots against his legitimate brother, Edgar, in his quest for power.

The torment began one Saturday, fifteen days after the devastating review. I stumbled through my lines during the storm, saving what was left of my voice for the final scene. No one was listening anyway. The cast left the stage with their infamous thunder sheets, I breathed a sigh of relief and was led by Arlindo—the Fool—and Claudio Melo—the Duke of Kent—to the trunk simulating a hut. Lineu and Paulo, Gloucester and Edgar, appeared stage right, a pair of noble pariahs. The young heartthrob Paulo Macedo, an excellent actor no one took seriously because he'd done three soap operas in a row in the same role of idiot, had accepted the challenge, believing the theater would change the course of his career. It did not. He requested a substitute soon after the premiere in São Paulo. He'd been invited to play the lead on a seven o'clock TV series and a lifetime contract compelled him to accept. He was right to do it, because our run came to an end while he was still with us, before we could try out another actor. And even if we had gone on: what chance did Shakespeare stand against the seven o'clock soap?

Paulo and Lineu came onstage in diapers like two Hindu mystics—the costume designer had made them specially for the cliff scene, in which the loyal son rescues his blind father from suicide. Lineu came toward me, groping about, feigning blindness by rolling his eyes back in his head until all you could see were the whites. I worried he'd end up with a detached retina, but he was one of those actors who gave everything to his craft. The duo comes upon the trio composed of Lear, the Fool, and the Duke, lost in the frigid expanse.

That was the moment it all fell apart.

Gloucester comes onstage, carried by Edgar, an anguished expression on the young actor's face, forced to endure the stench coming from his bathing-averse colleague. We'd made it through a good chunk of the scene when Paulo started in, right on cue, *Pillicock sat on Pillicock-hill, Halloo, halloo, loo, loo!* and began flapping his wings, imitating a cock as he feigned madness.

I was suddenly beset by an out-of-body experience.

My spirit left me, admiring from a distance that beautiful young man in his diaper, running around like a winged monkey. *How awful it would feel to watch a son humiliate himself like that*, I thought. In the audience, those who weren't asleep also watched aghast. I turned back to poor old Lineu rolling his eyes like he was Carmen Miranda, and I felt pity for Claudio, swimming in his sheepskin stole, sweat pouring down his temples. *Stop everything*, I begged in silence. *Stop the ride, I want to get off.*

It was the diapers, the diapers and Lineu feigning blindness, the sickening sight of the young heartthrob covered in his comrade's bodily fluids, the genius director and his sheet-metal thunder, my failing voice, me on all fours in the cubicle in Copacabana, the heartburn from the chicken, the pervert fireman, the scorched-earth reviews, the bewildered audience, the vultures circling the box office, the shopping mall swarming with people chasing winter clearances, my treacherous conscience, the fickle nature of the profession. I focused my attention on the threadbare curtain, I remembered just how much I hated Ivete Maria's offensive Regan, and I rued my idiotic delusion that I was up to the task of playing Lear. An elderly man in the first row had a coughing fit and his wife opened her purse to fish out a lozenge. The noise of the wrapper layered on to the husband's spasms, and someone whispered an angry *shhhh*. The pressure escaped from my diaphragm, the air rose up through my pharynx and paused in my mouth, forcing the upward contraction of my lips. I tried to stifle a laugh. *This cold night will turn us all to fools and madmen*, Arlindo said; *Take heed o' the foul fiend*, Paulo continued, and then they both turned to me. I ought to say something, but what? What? I couldn't even remember what act we were in. I'd totally blanked. I stood there, completely out of character, unable to move. Someone whispered a cue, I tried repeating it, but when I spoke my voice squeaked, choked off by my muffled laughter. You could see the panic stamped across the four idiots' foreheads. I lost it. Out came the laughter—I couldn't hold it, couldn't stop, overcome with a childish, demented, diabolic joy. I feigned madness for a second, I regained the bard's gravitas, but then it was worse, peals of laughter burst forth with renewed force, filling the auditorium, strong enough to double me over. I put my hands on my knees. *I'm sorry*, I said, to Lineu, to Paulo, the audience. *I'm sorry.*

An actor's imaginary world is a delicate thing. Bent over there in the middle of the action, I looked for a sign, some thought to put an end to my cackling. Debt, the fear of cancer, my disastrous career, the Doctors Without Borders jingle. But the sadistic, inhuman snigger held its ground, indifferent to my appeals to reason. I tried again, more than once—a lead actor has no right to abandon ship—but as soon as I caught sight of the diapers I was plunged back down into the abyss. *The curtain, the curtain*, I begged. I could hear the murmurs of the audience, the cast rushed to my aid, someone handed me a glass of water. *I'll be fine*, I said, *I'll be fine*. I steadied my breathing as the rest of the troupe looked on in horror. The audience began to clap in sync, demanding our return. In agony, I appealed to rage, I took a few kung fu leaps, feet and fists flying through the air. It was me against myself. My colleagues gave me some space. I unleashed a primal scream, then another, I exorcized whatever it was as best I could until I regained my senses. I came to a halt, sobered, out of breath. I held it together for two, three, four seconds. . . . *I'm good*, I said, *I'm good*. With a solemn air, I resumed my position at center stage. Lineu, Arlindo, Claudio, and Paulo took their places and I gave the order to open the curtain. The velvet was slowly drawn back, dust dancing in the stage lights, silence awaiting the resumption of the performance. The theater is a beautiful thing.

It lasted all of a second.

Another fit of laughter set in, I have no idea how we made it to the end. And again the next day—I made three attempts, one after the other, the curtain opening and closing as jaws dropped. I stopped the show, I gave the audience their money back, and left the theater still dressed as Lear. That night, sitting in my room at a cheap hotel, the only place willing to swap rooms for tickets, I cried until I had no more tears then passed out. I woke up in a panic, knowing that that very night I would have to face Lineu and Paulo in diapers, and that damn cock. I spent the entire performance in a cold sweat, my belly churning with anxiety. When the storm passed, Claudio and Arlindo led me to the hut and then Paulo came in with Lineu on his back. I tried not to look at the two of them, I delivered my lines facing the other way, but how to cover my ears? *Pillicock sat on Pillicock-hill, Halloo, halloo, loo, loo.* Another burst of laughter. Another night ruined. Sobs in the dressing room. The problem was becoming chronic. I asked to switch out the costumes, they covered themselves in doublets. That only made matters worse. I couldn't get the diapers out of my mind. We cut the rooster's speaking parts, but at that point it was automatic. The minute I sat on the throne, my lungs gave way. It took three weeks and a note in the newspaper before I threw in the towel. The final laugh attack took place before an audience of twenty-two paying customers. I was giggling from the start, completely helpless, and at the slightest provocation. I cut the first act short soon after Ivete Maria declared her deep love for her father. She was absolutely terrible, it was like she was being dubbed. I glanced over at Arlindo, he lowered his head and began to quiver. It was contagious. The curtain came down with the whole cast doubled over laughing, infected with a lack of faith that had begun with me. I went to the hotel to forget it all. In the dark of the hotel room, I didn't bother to count the drops of anxiety meds I squirted on my tongue, the whole endeavor had left me immune. I lay down on the sagging mattress and planned out my next steps. I would withdraw the money I had in the bank (what was left of my last TV contract), I'd pay what I owed to the team, the fine from the theater, the ads I'd already scheduled, the airfares, I would write a letter to the sponsor accepting responsibility and would go to Brasília to personally offer my mea culpa to the Ministry of Culture. I would give up the profession if I could figure out some other way to make a living. A restaurant, an inn on the coast, who knows, Paraty. Forget it, I thought, tomorrow I'll figure out what to do with myself. I crashed on the nylon sheets, rocked to sleep by the bard's words.

> *Vex not his ghost: O, let him pass! He hates him much*
> *That would upon the rack of this tough world*
> *Stretch him out longer.*

That was the end of Laughing Lear.

THE PHONE KEPT RINGING. I woke up out of sorts and it took a minute before I could figure out where I was. I yelled *Coming!* to no one in particular and stumbled across the room. When I reached the bathroom sink, standing there before the mirror, the king's eyes with their dark circles stared back at me. I wanted to die as my thoughts returned to the disaster. I stood there, still in makeup, tottering between two worlds. The ringing wouldn't stop and I let out another annoyed *Coming!*, turning over every last inch of that pigsty until I found the handset tossed behind the sofa. I picked up. The call was from Rio. A husky voice identified itself as that of Deputy Fire Chief Melo, from the 17th Division of the Copacabana Firemen's Corp.

Catastrophes travel in packs.

An old white lady who looked to be about eighty, hair dyed blonde, had been found nude, nearly drowned, on the beach in front of Rua Miguel Lemos. After going through her cell phone, found among her belongings scattered across the sand, they'd identified the last number dialed. *Do you know someone by the name of Maria Amélia Pires Cardoso, sir? Indeed I do*, I responded, *she's my mother, is everything all right? Yes, she's out of danger but a bit confused*, the voice said. *We took her to the emergency room at*

Hospital Miguel Couto, the voice continued. *I'm in São Paulo, I'm her only son, my mother's a widow*, I explained, suddenly aware of my own orphanhood. *Is there some relative or neighbor who is able to come get her? No . . . no . . . Aunt Neusa*, I thought, but then thought better of it. I promised to take the first flight out and then hung up, still in shock.

My old shortness of breath.

I sat on the bed, on the verge of losing it. But I was a grown man, I needed to suck it up. I grabbed a paper bag from the floor, stuck nose and mouth inside, and began to breathe at a steady pace. I'd seen it done in some film, perhaps it really worked. The paper bag inflated and deflated several times as I struggled to compose my thoughts. I crumpled the bag and tossed it away, asthma attack be damned. I wanted to take a shower, but it felt frivolous. I removed the streaks of makeup across my face with the tiny bar of soap next to the sink, stuffed what I could into my suit jacket, and fled like a man possessed, leaving the hotel bill, the cast, the theater, my career, the future. *Aeroporto Congonhas!* I barked at the taxi driver.

In all, it took me five hours to get from São Paulo to my destination. Bottlenecks, air traffic, turbulence, panic. I was a wreck by the time I made it to the public hospital, Miguel Couto. A packed emergency room, blood and wailing down the length of the hallway. True suffering. I was struck by a terrible sense of guilt when I saw my mother lying there on the stretcher behind a grimy curtain. When she saw me, she reached out her arms and flashed a relieved smile. I took her in my arms while she, holding on to my neck, whispered that she had known that I'd come back for her one day. Then she kissed me on the mouth. I wasn't sure what to make of the kiss or her comment, but I didn't want to stay there any longer than we had to. I signed the release papers and bolted for the private Hospital Samaritano in Botafogo. On the way, I scheduled a meeting with the family clinic. My mother was aloof about it all, clasping me the whole time, admiring the sliver of light peeping through the rear window of the taxi. I, on the other hand, felt tense, thinking about her, and about myself.

Dona Maria Amélia was an independent lady, she lived alone and made a point of not putting anyone else out. Recently, I'd noted a change in her behavior, sometimes she'd get days of the week mixed up, or forget that a friend had died, but nothing that necessitated a new routine. Now the conversation had taken a turn. The doctor who greeted me at the emergency room at Miguel Couto recommended we get an opinion from a neurologist.

As we drove past the Botanical Garden, my mother sat up in her seat, peered worriedly toward the street, then turned to me. She asked who would pick her son up from school. *What son?* I asked. *What do you mean, what son?* she asked. *Our son.* An icy chill came over my heart, a threatening sense of abandonment, as though I were standing before a ghost. The taxi had just passed the site of my old school next to the Parque Lage. The school had been torn down to make way for a ghastly mirrored-glass tower. *Mom*, I contested, *I'm your son.* Her cheeks immediately sagged. She looked at me with horror on her face, then she turned away in an attempt to ensure that the school still existed. But the traffic lurched forward, leaving the problem behind. Spaced out, for a minute she didn't move. Then, she nestled up against my arm and never mentioned the subject again. Terrified, I too kept quiet.

We made it to the Hospital Samaritano in the early evening. The neurology team, which would be taking care of my mother's exams, showed up only after ten. My mother vanished amid a throng of doctors, and I sat in the café trying to think of some merciful soul who could come to my rescue. I downed three espressos in a row. I needed every one. My marriage of fifteen years had ended badly with Marta driven from the house after an outrageous argument. We never spoke again. Our lack of children facilitated a clean break without regrets, something I had long treated as a source of pride. At that moment, not so much. My mother liked Marta. Our former maid, who had worked for the family ever since I could remember, had died two months earlier, a heart attack. I suspected that her absence, the absence of a lifelong companion, had contributed to the Maria Amélia's sudden confusion. Aunt Neusa, my father's little sister, and the cousins, her children, were the only relatives to whom I could appeal. My mother, an only child, had no one. I hadn't seen the rest of them since my grandmother, a tiny woman of nearly a hundred from Minas Gerais, had entered orbit, drifting between worlds. They were all still there, in Tijuca as they had always been, but I wouldn't know what to ask, or say. I took the cell phone from my pocket, but I didn't have the nerve. Instead of calling, I did something I hadn't done for more than two years: I bummed a cigarette from the guy sitting next to

21

me, asked for a light from the driver near the entrance, and felt endless relief as I breathed in the toxic smoke. *God, it's nice to slowly kill yourself*, I thought, conscious of being responsible, in light of my lack of children, for the total extinction of my line.

I slept badly on the pull-out couch. My mother woke up with her face aglow. When she saw me stumble out of the bathroom, she asked for a good morning kiss. I gave her a hug, afraid of her. Maria Amélia offered her lips, I offered my cheek, this little joust stretched for three interminable seconds, until she asked whether something had gone wrong between us. I thought about repeating that I wasn't married to her, but I didn't want to get her worked up. I accepted my role as husband and answered with a vague *It's nothing, honey*, claiming I hadn't brushed my teeth. She let out a naughty little laugh. The nurse arrived to deliver me, sparing us any further awkwardness. At breakfast, I turned my attention to the funeral of another victim of senility, my King Lear.

†

Thrown to the lions, Milena, my producer, started screaming as soon as she picked up the phone. The other actors had been barred from leaving the hotel, their luggage impounded until the bill was settled. They'd begun picketing at the reception desk. *Where are you, Mario? Lineu had a conniption in the lobby*, she added, still reeling. The troupe's protest echoed in the background. I explained the scare my mother had given me, pleaded that it was Sunday, that there was no way for me to transfer the money, I promised to try, but it was held up in investments. *Put the manager on*, I told her. The man listened patiently before responding that he was sorry, but the luggage would be returned only when all expenses were paid. The producer grabbed the telephone again, she was afraid that Paulo, the heartthrob from the seven o'clock soap, would hit her. *It's best you speak to him*, she said. The rude voice of a wounded alpha male spouted curses from the other end of the line. I tried to arouse some pity in him, but Paulo preferred to trade insults; I got fed up, hung up on him, and went out to clear my head. I bummed my second cigarette in less than twenty-four hours and tried, one more time, to make the transfer, without success. I needed to put out the fire in São Paulo, but the doctors were threatening to discharge Maria Amélia. I inhaled deeply, so that the puffs of nicotine reached the roots of the alveoli, and reflected on how life was a bitch.

†

I was happy in the beginning, at age twenty, and again at thirty, when I left the theater behind and put together a string of TV hits. Having reached fame, I lived at the height of arrogance. I screwed a lot, spent more than I should have, humiliated understudies, I believed in fate. Not anymore. A fat contract transformed me into a lazy actor. Over the years, I tired of the taping routine and accepted bit parts. One day, a young actor, the darling of the moment, the kind that are still willing to take risks, looked at my well-established belly, my pronounced widow's peak, and confided ironically: *You know, Mario, it's been proven, life exists beyond television.*

I felt humiliated by these pubescent certainties. *Why not take on new risks?* I thought. Middle age is a period of negligence and uncertainty in a man's life. In a woman's, too, but their challenges, at least, can be chalked up to hot flashes, hormonal depression that justifies their poor decision-making. A man, no, he carries on the same as he always was, only worse, worse with each passing day, rinsing his hair with color-treatment shampoos when no one can see and falling hard for girls young enough to be his daughters. Women are more realistic. Nature demands it.

I made the crazy decision to quit. The rest is history. Long story short: there I was, at the door of the hospital, newly wedded to my mother, owing money I didn't have on account of my thinly veiled ambition to become Laurence Olivier of the Jungle.

†

Immersed in thought, I barely noticed the physician arrive. *Cigarettes won't help*, he said, with the swagger reserved for members of the white-jacket caste. I reacted like a brat caught red-handed by the school hall monitor and flicked the cig to the ground. He laughed a chiding laugh. Ashamed, I picked up my litter and found the nearest trash receptacle. The meeting was quick. The diagnosis, worrisome. Maria Amélia was suffering from some degenerative brain disease that wasn't Alzheimer's, but which would worsen with time. *She won't suffer*, the doctor assured me, *it's more difficult for those looking in from outside*. I wanted to throw my arms around him, cry on a sympathetic

24

shoulder, but doctors frown on such forms of self-pity. I limited myself to objective queries. *My mother's been confusing me with my father, I don't know what to do*, I admitted, *I don't want to see her unhappy. Do what's most comfortable for you and for her*, came Dr. Know-It-All's vague response. *Just don't leave her on her own*, he concluded.

He had other cases to deal with, as bad or worse than mine. I managed to convince him to delay discharge until the following day. As soon as the doctor turned his back I ran to the closest bar, bought a pack of cigarettes, and went back to smoking like a chimney. My phone was vibrating hysterically, it was the producer. Did no one in the entire cast have a mother? I didn't answer, doing as a friend had advised: when someone brings you a problem, turn your back and walk away. Faithful to the maxim, I forgot São Paulo and focused on Tijuca. Aunt Neusa was my only hope of finding someone to take care of Maria Amélia in Rio while I put out *Lear*'s fire in São Paulo.

I SET OFF from the hospital late in the afternoon, soon after the game began between Vasco and Flamengo at Maracanã Stadium. It was the best way to avoid traffic, unfeasible moments before the ball began rolling across the grass. I could have left earlier but I didn't want to linger on this visit. It had been more than three years since I'd seen the family. I was afraid of what I'd find.

I grabbed a taxi and we headed toward the Rebouças tunnel.

Rebouças is one long curve without natural light; the entrance disappears and the end refuses to arrive. We crossed the opening and the yellow lights made the transition from day to the exhaust-filled darkness. Immediately, I felt the pressure of the tons of rock above of my head, the layers of stone that separated me from the Redeemer. I was convinced the tunnel was about to collapse. This was an old fear, dating back to the time when the overpass came crashing down. I had been getting ready for a lunch at my grandmother's house when the first images appeared on the television screen. An entire segment of Avenida Paulo de Frontin had fallen atop cars passing through the neighborhood of Catumbi. A half-hour earlier, and I would have been a victim of the tragedy. Ever since, I had developed a terror of such roadways that, over the years, had restricted itself to the tunnel. The shortness of breath never left me. I typically avoided the route altogether but that day, given the urgency, I decided to risk it.

The taxi stopped at the extremity of the dead-end street hidden behind Praça Saens Peña. Aunt Neusa always swore that the square, before the tragedy that was the subway's arrival, had been the life of Tijuca. But ever since they'd opened up that hole, the dust and unbearable heat never let up from January through December, making intelligent life all but impossible in the Ipanema of the Northern Boroughs. The trees had died, the movie theaters were shuttered, the Palheta Cafe, the Sears stores, what remained of the '50s had given way to blocks of cheap concrete, bottlenecks, and teenage hooligans with glass shards in hand.

When it was time to pay for the ride, the driver requested a photo, he was a fan. I flashed an annoyed smile, he took the selfie, and I slammed the door shut on my way out. He was angry. He had reason to be. Insulted, the young man screeched his tires as he backed out, he'd placed stickers on the windows as a reminder, but rare was the passenger who took into the consideration the costs of maintaining a car. I certainly didn't. I opened the gate and stepped onto the flagstones where I'd spent much of my childhood. I took the service stairwell, a narrow labyrinth that snaked around the three-floor building from the outside. The uneven steps made the climb arduous, even for adult legs. After scaling the wall, I caught a glimpse of the stream, an open-air sewer that enclosed the rear of the modest building. As a kid, I would train my aim throwing rocks at the rats that would scurry across the passageway chasing the sun. They were still there, in larger numbers than before, but the vegetation had retreated and a recent cement pipe had covered the stream that ran in the space abutting the opposite lot.

My grandmother lived on the third, and last, floor with my widowed aunt and the grandchildren who had never left home. The kitchen door had been left open, I walked in without warning. The butter was still dripping over the plastic tablecloth, the smell of trash, the hydraulic tiles, and the collection of cooking-oil cans with their edges flattened to prevent accidents accumulated beneath the sink, God knows why.

Aunt Neusa appeared from the living room. When she saw me, she let out a childish gasp, standing before the nephew she hadn't seen for centuries. She was the runt of the litter, as my grandmother liked to say. She was born with a jolt, when my father was just entering adolescence. She was fifteen years older than I was, but looked much older. Beneath her white hair and missing teeth, my aunt still had a girlish air, wearing tight Lycra shorts that went to the knee, ankle socks, and a Unimed T-shirt. When she'd recovered from the shock, she invited me in. She headed for the table in the tiny living room, holding my arm, overjoyed at having someone to talk to.

My grandfather's old office, reconfigured as a bedroom as the generations squeezed in, was the only sleeping quarters directly connected to the living room. I could sense my grandmother's presence in the shadow of the door. I got spooked. I spooked easily.

After offering me a chair, Aunt Neusa returned to the kitchen and started in with her ear-splitting jabber, a hodge-podge of *When are you going to do more soaps* and *Matias earned a medal for his swimming*. I asked for some water to occupy Baby Jane, that was what I called her, and kept my gaze on the dark crack in the door. She came back with the cups, reciting her grandson's schedule: English, judo, soccer. The ex-girlfriend of her thirty-something son did not want to raise the child. Even better, it now fell to his grandmother to worry about the homework, the baths, and the end-of-year presentations. With her children, everything had gone wrong, but now, with the young boy, she once again held hope that life would be a walk on the beach. The subject turned to the old lady's condition. A resigned look on her face, Aunt Neusa gave a rundown of her mother's day.

"She woke up, hungry, at nine, I gave her some oatmeal, her Imosec, and then she went back to bed. At noon, she complained she was feeling nauseous but she ate a bit of chicken soup and half a pear. Just now, I went back to look. . . ."

Aunt Neusa paused for a moment and I was certain she would finish her sentence with *and then she died*. My throat began to seize up as I was again assailed by shortness of breath. *If that's the case*, I thought, *I'll run and throw myself from the window*. The pool at the Tijuca Tennis Club, games of tag on the ground floor, Carnaval street parties, the World Cups, the golden hour of my nostalgia, everything I once knew to be happiness, ended there, with Tijuca's own Doris Day looking after her deceased mother.

I regretted taking the tunnel.

All my departed relatives had died while I was away, without exception. I even escaped the stroke that took my father, who left this world with me at a safe distance, during a tour in Recife, selling out theaters with *The Imaginary Invalid*. I always nurtured the belief that my mother was immortal. But there, as my Aunt Neusa came up for breath, I feared that, on that fateful afternoon, destiny would make me responsible for the postmortem care of the matriarch. Violins, a casket, flowers, the whole horde of family members. Would it all fall to me? What about the neighbors? What about all my cousins without jobs?

"Just now, I looked in on her again," she said, "and she's awake. You want to go see her?"

My relief at having narrowly escaped the planning of burial rites lasted less than a second before the terror of finding myself face-to-face with the ghost seized my entire being. No, I didn't want to go see. See what? The last time I'd seen my grandmother she couldn't even recognize me. What was I doing there? My aunt already had to double down to take care of her own mother. Maria Amélia was my problem. I took another drink of water, I'd only just arrived, I couldn't just leave. There was no escaping the grave. I decided to fake it, it was the only morally acceptable solution.

"Yes, I'd really like to see her," I responded solemnly.

In a vulgar move, I forced my aunt to take the lead, my hands clasping her hunched shoulders from behind, as though to defend against some threat. We walked in. The afternoon sun against the closed shade produced vapors like a Turkish bath. Aunt Neusa turned on the lamp. *Want to open a window?* I was about to suggest, but then I remembered the family's asepsis, the dread of germs that guided their every move. At age seven, with the flu, I was sent to bed and covered with sheets. They locked the house as though battling the plague. A shower? Only in the event of fever; to protect against a draft, they repeated. I was growing visibly worse during this internment until my parents came to the rescue and cured me with fresh air. I thought of doing the same thing with my grandmother, saving her, taking her from there to die in Prague, Venice, places it hadn't even occurred to those in Tijuca might exist. But no, I wouldn't do that. Forget Venice. If God were just, an hour from then I would be on the other side of the tunnel, with my grandmother where she'd always been, between the subway station at Praça Saens Peña and the Favela do Borel.

While I planned my escape, Aunt Neusa was trying to make contact with my ailing grandmother, who was present only in the physical sense. Her sunken eyes peered inward, as though admiring an invisible landscape. To my astonishment, she was smiling. Sensing she was about to receive visitors, she had begun to mumble a few confused words, directed not at me or her daughter but at people who were no longer there. With great effort, her withered lips managed to string a sentence together. She wanted to know if her sister had left the message. *Did Alzira leave the message?* she repeated. Her daughter responded affirmatively, the message was given, as she turned to me, making a crazy sign with her finger.

31

I thought back to Lear's madness. I should have studied my grandmother more closely, rather than wasting my time on all fours with the speech coach in Copacabana.

Aunt Neusa lowered her voice and explained that I had come to visit, JORGE'S SON, she said in an optimistic tone, as though the fact might bring her mother some joy. But neither Jorge nor Neusa existed wherever my grandmother was. My best guess was her parents' backyard, in the neighborhood of Méier, with all her siblings and cousins, all deceased. She didn't remember ever marrying, she had no memory of her children, but described the ribbon in her sister's hair and the stone columns beneath the front porch, she knew the name of the dog and the cat. Some time ago, she had left behind her cluttered bedroom on the dead-end street adjacent to Praça Saens Peña and had moved back to the house that had been her parents'. I, her adult grandson, frozen there at the foot of the bed, meant nothing to her.

The indifference was mutual.

My grandmother tired of her delirium and dozed off. My eyes took a quick survey of the vestiges of prosperity. The small shrine, the bookshelf with my grandfather's law textbooks, the jacaranda furniture, as alive to me as my flesh-and-blood relatives. Patiently, I waited for Aunt Neusa to give the order to retreat.

If I were able to describe the relief I felt at returning to the kitchen table, what a poem it would be! I drank the rest of my water, my aunt served coffee, and the lack of things to talk about seized us both. I didn't have the courage to tell her what I was doing there. The cicadas were singing, the orange afternoon bathed the side of a neighboring building, and Aunt Neusa took to gathering up the cookie crumbs scattered across the table. Accustomed to finding refuge in household chores, she put an end to the awkward situation by asking whether I wouldn't like something to eat. *I've got bread, I've got cheese, I've got a banana*. I smiled, thankful for the subtle way she had sidestepped our silence. I suddenly remembered the tender feelings I'd always had for her.

"I'd have a banana," I answered.

Aunt Neusa went to grab one.

The fireworks crackled, voices shouting *Gol, Flamengo*, the Vultures had done it again. The commotion added a bit of festive spirit to the occasion. Aunt Neusa returned from the kitchen with a bunch of bananas in her hands, looking upset.

"Oh, my Lord! The game!"

She ran for the remote control for the 40-inch TV, the only modern luxury in the house. The green shone brightly on the screen, the pitch still smoky from the celebration.

"How did I forget? Marcelo and Cynthia left dressed like the devil. Carine's wearing a cardboard box on her belly pretending it's a television. She wrote GALVÃO, OVER HERE. Could they already have showed up on the TV? The whole group's at a bar around the corner, waiting to see them."

She sat down with her face glued to the screen, worried she'd lost her offspring's five seconds of fame. Carine, Marcelo, and Cynthia, she told me, had spent the week in Madureira piecing together their outfits. To draw more attention, the couple had chosen big horns and curly blond nylon wigs. Carine had a cardboard box from the supermarket and then a light-bulb went off. She cut out the screen, pinned it to suspenders, and threw on her bikini, her belly painted green to imitate the pitch.

"Do you think they already showed them?"

Her desperation revived my own anxiety. I prayed for Carine and Marcelo to appear on the screen. Consoling Aunt Neusa would be even more painful than burying my grandmother.

Vasco went on the attack, but it made no difference. The poor thing's eyes ran back and forth across the specks in the bleachers, searching for the golden locks. I summoned my strength. *At least I don't need to make conversation*, I thought, focusing on the monitor. Ten minutes of obsession passed, Aunt Neusa could no longer take it, and shot up from the couch.

"I'm going to call Alfredo."

She opened her tattered address book, which hung on a hook in the hallway leading to the bedrooms, where the landline could be found. She dialed.

"You remember him? Little Fredo? He lived on José Higino. . . ." she was about to continue before someone picked up on the other side. "Fredo?! I can't hear a thing. IT'S ME . . . AUNTIE NEUSA. . . . !"

Her children's friends called her Auntie.

"Did they show up yet?" she asked hesitantly. "THANK GOD!" and she wagged her finger: negative. Next, still agitated, she hung up and resumed her vigil. I relaxed on the plastic seat cushion and, free from the obligation to demonstrate compassion, dedicated my attention to the game. Given that I was a Fluminense fan, I rooted for Vasco, even though they were losing. I would leave right after the final whistle.

†

Carine dated Rogério, got engaged to Rogério, took seven years to marry Rogério, and fewer than two to divorce Rogério. *Irreconcilable Differences*, the court documents read. They fought nonstop. *Are you kidding me?* Her failure accepted, my cousin once again crammed in the family shoebox with her brother, her sister-in-law-of-the-moment, her nephew and his ex, her mother, and her grandmother. Beer took the place of Nesquik, the evening soap, the cartoons, and life went on.

Be fruitful and multiply. And that's what they did.

Not infrequently, I envied their lack of ambition, the simplistic existence of my relatives, their capacity for wild enthusiasm for the most mundane things: from the collection of bottle caps to the car of the year, from Frosted Flakes to gourmet margarine. They lived for the year's major events, ecstatic at the Christmas ads, the season premiere of the latest soaps, the New Year's addresses, and Carnaval parades. They idolized sports stars like Bernardinho, Senna, and Romário. They discussed the new opening to the TV program *Fantástico*. Everyone else's joy was theirs, too, since in practice they had little reason to celebrate themselves.

It must be wonderful to be like that, I used to think, alternating between repugnance for their vegetative state and mourning the loss of my bygone innocence.

Over the years, Tijuca, which had given me so much, became a distant memory, losing all personal meaning. But now, admiring the view from the veranda, the small houses that still maintained the elegance of the past, rare survivors of the neighborhood's decline, I had misgivings about my coolness. That forgotten corner of Rio brought endless nostalgia. The dead-end street, my childhood, my cousins, the tenderness of my grandmother and my father when he was still alive. A longing. For being a child, for having a mother.

†

Walter Casagrande took over the play-by-play, the camera scanned the stands, and then, suddenly, my three cousins appeared on screen. I jumped out of my seat together with Aunt Neusa. Throwing our arms around each other, it was as if we were celebrating a goal. Marcelo, Cynthia, and Carine, going nuts in a desperate frenzy to show up on TV, proudly posed in their scanty outfits. The girls shook their beer bellies and my cousin, a tank, wore a pair of Speedos and a red cape tied around his neck. Blond, all three of them. Carine, moored to her cardboard television, was the first to notice her own image on the stadium screen. The three of them pointed and then searched for the nearest camera. They howled with delight. It was the pinnacle of their existence. Marcelo formed a heart by cupping his two hands and screamed *I LOVE YOU, MOM* for Neusa to hear. Then it cut to commercials.

My aunt nearly fainted. She cried and moaned, going wild on the roll-out couch. She asked for her blood pressure medication, she couldn't take it. I ran to the house's only bathroom, grabbed the vial from the medicine cabinet and, dizzied, bound back to the living room. Would hers be the body I'd end up burying that day?

The incursion into the old familiar hallway had a lingering effect. While I rushed to Aunt Neusa's aid with a glass of water and her pills in hand, I retraced the steps I'd just taken. The door of the master bedroom on the right, the furniture unchanged since the day they were married, the leaky bathroom on the left, and two bedrooms at the end of the hall, which I didn't dare approach. Everything smaller, much smaller than I remembered it. Two old women, three adults, a child, and centuries of junk crammed into a thousand square feet.

Only the escapism, I reflected, the grinning idiocy of the variety shows, to help those living there hang on.

Aunt Neusa survived the flood of emotion. Regaining her composure, she picked up the telephone. It was Alfredo. Proud of his friend's accomplishment, he was screaming on the other end of the line. *This family knows how to produce artists*, she said into the receiver, shooting a knowing glance in my direction. She thanked Fredo for his words, basked in the glory of filial devotion, and beamed as she hung up, as though she'd just married off a daughter.

We watched the game until the end, but it wasn't any fun. I heard, without paying attention, about Cynthia's plans to take the civil servants' exam for the city government and about Marcelo's difficulties with the manager of the sporting goods store on Rua Uruguai, where he worked. *Carine still isn't over the divorce*. That was my aunt's way of explaining why my cousin wasn't going to school, wasn't working, and also wasn't doing anything about it. *She looks after Matias now and then*, and then she stopped. I didn't go on about myself either. No goal, no expulsion, no ugly fouls. The small talk dragged on for another twenty, thirty minutes, before the apartment regained its usual melancholy. The cold light of the ceiling lamp, the yellowed walls, the visible decay.

It was time to go. I had no right to ask anything of her.

Aunt Neusa insisted that I stay until my cousins returned from the game, but I said I had a meeting early the next morning in São Paulo. It wasn't a lie. *Are you going to go back to doing soaps?* she asked me again. *I don't know, I don't think so.* She let out a disappointed sigh. *And Amélia, how is she?* my aunt wanted to know. I faltered, I nearly told her my real reason for being there, I nearly begged for help, but I stayed quiet. *She's great*, I said, *she said to send you a kiss. Tell her I'm sending her one too*, my aunt replied tenderly. Then she dragged me back to the bedroom where her ailing mother lay. Resigned, I followed her, kissed my grandmother's gelid hand, and ran out of there as fast as I could. I fumbled down the stairs to the ground floor, the smell of ammonia assaulting my nostrils, my feet hit the sidewalk, and I thanked God for the problems I had.

NIGHT HAD JUST FALLEN. The newly lit streetlamps still flickered weakly. The gusting warm air forecasted rain. The two blocks that stood between me and the square turned sinister after nightfall. I quickened my pace. The worst thing about this city is the fear of turning the corner.

An argument and a group saying "knock it off" came down the crosswalk. Further ahead, I noticed the mob of fans pouring out into the street. It was the post-game crowd. I froze. My mother in the hospital became a distant reality. I should have left in the middle of the second half. The swarm of amped-up drones, the flag-toting cars honking on their victory parade, the savagery of Rio at full tilt. I considered hiding in an alley until things died down, ducking into a lobby, anything but going back to my aunt's house. Two guys performed the small miracle of hailing a taxi a few feet from where I was, the scene revived my hopes of escape. I marched down the street, everything was full. A bus, packed to the gills at the nearest stop, shook to the sound of Zulu drums. Biceps, hanging out the windows, banged against the metal exterior. People flooded out from the robo-centipede. A couple got out of a rickety old taxi, I ran in their direction, but three delinquents grabbed the door one second after I did. I'd gotten there first, there was no denying that, but they didn't want to hear it. One got in through the opposite door, the other two through the other, and told the driver to hit it. I'm not used to being a victim of injustice. I'm a sensitive actor with an ailing mother. The insult in plain daylight, coming from some asshole with rock-hard abs, wounded my delicate constitution. Standing on the curb, I was overcome with shortness of breath. I wasn't like them, I didn't have the constitution to put up with such barbarity, the lack of manners on that late night in the Praça Saens Peña. It wasn't the Tijuca I had known.

I caught sight of a yellow Voyage at the stoplight on the opposite corner, I tried to walk to it, but the blood had left my legs. Wobbling, I traced a line toward the rooftop light: TÁXI, and I set off running like a madman. I pulled the door handle, got in without looking to either side, and sat down, leaning against the front seat. Keeled over in the tight space, my eyes glued to the tattered floor rug, I noticed two short legs near my ear flinch in fear. I looked to my right and saw a spruced-up boy of five or six, his bulging eyes staring at me. The door opened on his side and two dark-skinned arms pulled him out; I lifted my head, the arms reached back in, and an outraged face came toward me. The voice, the teeth, the beauty, the breath of that woman; her expressive face speaking words I couldn't understand. A shrill cry interrupted my momentary muteness and her words suddenly became intelligible.

"Do you have no shame?" She was asking me if I was ashamed. "Get out! Get out, I'm telling you!"

She wanted me to get out. I tried to explain it was a mis-understanding, it was about to rain, I had seen the taxi, I was feeling sick, my mother needed me; *my life's at risk out there*, I tried to explain, but she wouldn't listen. The wind picked up and the first drops of rain hit the windshield. Protecting her younglings under her wings, she demanded I retreat.

It was only then that I saw there were two children.

The girl looked at me like one of the Three Little Pigs staring at the Big Bad Wolf. Clinging to her nanny's skirt, she clenched her tiny hands in a state of shock. The boy hid behind the young woman's legs. I was willing to own up, but not to the point of moving my ass. Trying to be friendly, I proposed a compromise. I would pay the fare but we'd split the cab.

"We can drop the three of you off first," I said.

"Get out," she insisted.

The nerve, the haughtiness. I wished all sorts of evil to be visited upon that woman. Was I not being fair? I'm very calm until someone pushes my buttons. The time for conversation was over. I left the three of them outside the taxi, slammed the door, and barked at the driver.

"Head to Copacabana!"

The Voyage didn't budge. The driver, I noticed only then, was an enormous mixed-race man whose shoulders were, by quite a margin, wider than the driver's seat. The giant turned toward me with a stern expression. Without taking his hands from the wheel, he spoke slowly and deliberately.

"I'm going to give you to the count of three to get out of my car. I ain't going anywhere with some prick who treats a woman like that."

The fear of getting a beating closed the bronchi once and for all. My head fell back, I sucked in the air as best I could. I was going to die. He started counting. *One . . . two. . . .* My hands slid toward my pants pocket, I grabbed my wallet, and offered all that I had. A hundred, two hundred, two twenty, two twenty-seven, twenty-eight. . . . I shoved the bills into his hand, I begged him to take me away. The Fridge stared at me without touching the money. I'd offended him. I awaited my punishment, the fateful count of three, but the mastodon only told me to look at the floor and quietly reflect on what I'd done. I resisted the urge to shield myself against his fists while calculating the hours I'd spent to earn the equivalent of that pile of paper.

"You're going to step out of this car," he said, "then you're going to apologize to the lady there, you're going to take the bags from her hand, the kids' bags and backpacks, you're going to put the suitcase in the trunk, hold the door for them to get in, you're going to sit right next to me here and keep quiet as a mouse until I drop you off on the other side of the tunnel. And you're going to write me a check now, twice the value of what you're offering. And the money stays as a down payment." He grabbed the banknotes and stashed them beneath the console.

I wrote a check with the help of a pen hanging from a string on a clipboard and handed it over. He read my name out loud.

"Mario Cardoso . . . I thought it was you. If this check bounces, Mr. Mario Cardoso, you can be sure I'll be at the door of the television studio, I'll make a point to go there personally to collect it." And he stuffed the check into his pocket.

I would have given my life to be a nobody.

The three other passengers hadn't moved. The oaf rolled down the window and explained our deal. I got out of the car and put their bags into the trunk. I tried to help the girl, but she let out a scream, thinking I was trying to steal her backpack. I didn't even try with the little guy. I opened the door with a bow, they got in, I sat in the front seat and breathed a sigh of relief. *Now, we just need to make it through the bottlenecks*, I thought.

The rain came crashing down at the Praça da Bandeira.

Within minutes, the sewers couldn't keep up with the torrent. We needed to reach the overpass before the road flooded. The ride had been tense, each of us looking out a different side of the car, keeping an eye on the gutters; the children closed their eyes, seized by the nightmare. The Paulo de Frontin, site of the greatest trauma of my youth, appeared on our right, the car pulled onto the ramp, and I relaxed fifty feet above the ground.

The driver switched on the radio to check the traffic and I saw, in the rearview mirror, the nanny and the *infantes* curled up in the corner behind him. She took a bottle of water from a plastic bag and gave it to the younger one. She did this while running her fingers through the little girl's hair. The boy gave the bottle back and leaned up against her arm again. The young woman looked outside and gazed at the night with a deep, lost look in her eyes.

It was someone like her that I needed.

The guard dog took note of my indiscretion, he turned the rearview mirror, and I faced front again. The mouth of the tunnel glowed brighter and brighter. Rebouças no longer scared me.

†

We parked in front of a building in the Jardim Botânico neighborhood. It was still raining. Without waiting for the command, I got out to render my services. I dumped their stuff at the reception and returned to help with the kids, who were out cold in the back seat. I offered to take the boy, but the nanny snarled at me, as though I were a pedophile, or worse. Her arrogance, once again, bothered me. The need to remember that she'd been wronged. *I've reached my quota*, I thought to myself, *I'm up to my neck with problems. If she doesn't want my help, I won't help. In fact, I don't even want to. Let's forget this whole unfortunate little episode occurred.* I didn't need to say anything more. She herself woke the little girl, grabbed a poncho to cover the boy, lifted him in her arms, and got out. I took off my soaking-wet jacket and covered the older one until we reached the building. Before walking inside, she turned to me and said with disgust:

"I used to really like you, sir, but now, every time I see your face on television, the first thing I'm going to do is change the channel."

The doorman opened the door and up they went, disappearing forever.

Leaning against the building's gate, I realized what a bastard I'd been. That woman, my cousins, my aunt, the crazy Tijuca I didn't recognize, they were my audience. People who would sell the family farm to avoid having to endure three hours of talk about a foolish English monarch, bad father, terrible regent, and arrogant madman who'd lost his kingdom for a horse. Life had made an idiot of me, and for what? *For Hecuba. And what is Hecuba to me, or I to Hecuba, that I should cry thus for her?* I should have stayed in television.

The taxi driver waited for me to approach the car. I tried to open the door, but it was locked. Othello rolled down the window, gave me a vengeful *ciao*, and sped off, tires screeching. Sopping wet in the dark street, I now believed in divine justice. It took me nearly three hours to get to the Hospital Samaritano. I overcame deep puddles, leptospirosis, traffic, and, without a taxi, two crammed buses. I paid a price for my arrogance. I deserved it.

My mother was already out. She'd had an anxiety attack in my absence and they'd given her a tranquilizer. I called the clinician and implored him to keep her in the hospital until Wednesday. I crashed. I dreamed of the nanny. She ran her hands through my hair in the back seat of a taxi.

†

The next day, I pulled out the money I'd invested and marched with sure steps to the airline check-in counter, ready to face ancient England in São Paulo. Thousands of people had fought hard, like me, to make it to the country's financial center. I bought the ticket, went through security, and sat down at my gate. I typed a message. *I made the transfer, I'm at the airport, on my way*. Sent. My telephone started vibrating in my pants pocket, it was the producer, I didn't pick up. I sat in seat 7B, between a businesswoman and a young man covered in tattoos. The dragon on his arm brandished its claws. *Bring it*, I thought, *I'm ready for you*. The Boeing picked up speed, the wheels lifted from the ground, we cut through the clouds until we reached space. How long had it been since I'd been happy? Too long, I thought.

I'D BEEN HAPPY in Paris, during the paid respite to rest my image after taking on the role of an odious villain, burned alive on national television. Augusto Reis deserved to die. A despot who married for money, cheated on his wife with his sister-in-law, switched out his own child in the maternity ward, and set in motion the death of the family matriarch, his own mother. Only Hell would do.

Augusto had exploded in a puddle-jumper mid-flight, a ball of fire ejected into space, clinging to the fortune he'd stolen from his business partners. The immolation drew 90 percent of the prime-time audience, a commercial break sold for the price of gold, and the program's cast were elevated to prime-time gods. In return, I got two first-class tickets to blow off some steam in the City of Lights and a fat new contract worthy of an Arabian sultan. I locked myself in my suite at the Plaza Athénée with Marta and we spent ten days living off the tasting menu. Just eating, drinking, fucking. Pure Epicurus! Back in Brazil, my collection of videocassettes had reached 157 titles. Brandos, De Niros, Mastroiannis, and Gassmans, I had them all. I liked to overindulge in whiskey, watching Bergman's Scandinavian ruminations. That satisfied

47

the intellectual ambitions I'd abandoned to do television. With an enviable ability to endure the heavy work of recording, I had no children and was living the peak of my marriage to a woman who would make any competitor envious. Not even I could handle her.

When I was starting out in the theater, we were all lefties, devotees of Brecht, Gorky, and Arrabal. Money was synonymous with bad character. But the world changed and my hard-up friends turned into trattoria pariahs, decked out in Bermuda shorts and flip-flops, they had no health insurance, no car, no prospects. They gave me the cold shoulder, but I'd hauled in quite the harvest.

My time off flew by. I missed the adoring fans. Late one warm December, I was invited to repeat my feat, to hold down the attraction that accounted for 40 percent of the organization's revenues: the eight o'clock soap. The creator wanted me to contend with the love of two beauties who could act to boot. Nothing could go wrong. Renato Brandão would die, murdered at the end of the first episode, and would reappear in the third, with another name, married to a young woman, striking confusion into the heart of the mature heroine, still in love with his deceased clone. Hitchcock's *Vertigo* served as inspiration. I took the Master of Suspense's collection off my shelf and studied the antics of Stewart and Grant. I boarded the plane for Europe acting like I'd signed with MGM. We began work in March, in the heavenly city of London, convinced we were reinventing film noir. Those were two weeks of binges, mutual flattery, and a bit of hard work in the London fog. The director did everything but kiss the crew on the mouth, so dazzled was he at the prospect of revolutionizing national television. At the cast party that preceded some time off, I dragged the older female lead to the bedroom and we embarked on a torrid secret romance. We returned to the studio convinced we were about to make history.

We fell back to earth a week after the show went on air.

The ratings report showed a descending curve and the bigwigs ordered some more polls. The rabble hadn't caught on to my character's death and resurrection. Housewives had mistaken suspense for spiritist drama, without understanding whether or not I was a ghost. All social strata rejected me. Condemned to limbo, Renato Brandão was ejected from the core to give the kids in the junior cast a step up. They honored the hefty salary, but the mature leading lady ended up in another heartthrob's arms. She never called me again. I was demoted to a nice middle-aged man, a club owner, who came onscreen to say he was on his way out.

I sat sitting spinning my wheels for what seemed like ages, waiting for declarations of undying love from the young cast in Studio D. I suffered nine months on the outs. On the street, everyone asked when I was going to go back to doing soaps. Everything that had distinguished me until then, my revolutionary past, my rebellious personality, my acerbic wit, everything that had brought me to Olympus was now a flaw and a limitation. I complained about how long things were taking, the roles, the costumes, I made no attempt to hide my disdain for the girls of fifteen who cried like rubber dolls. Yes, crying is

49

of supreme importance in TV, especially for an aspiring actress. What did their tragic way of speaking or total lack of culture matter if they could shed an honest tear? All of them knew it, too, and they took recourse to old tricks, their eyes bulging out of their heads as they stared into the mirror without blinking; smearing their cornea in Japanese crystal, risking, like Lineu, their vision as the price for professional success. Those who could cry without effort left me feeling hopeless. *It's a physiological phenomenon*, I thought, *that's the only explanation*. The young men had no need to appeal to tears, boys don't cry; if they weren't complete idiots and made the women blush, they would shine, in time.

But I'd failed as the ideal man. No one remembered Augusto Reis anymore, only the abject failure that was Renato Brandão, the reject protagonist. My situation demanded humility.

This time, I had no respite, I had no Paris, I had no fawning and flattering.

To salvage my contract, I followed up the fiasco with a supporting role on the six o'clock soap. The top brass advised me to accept. It was a period drama, taking place on a sugarcane plantation in colonial Brazil, complete with whipping posts. The slave-driver José Dias beat the hell out of half the cast, first coming on to the mestizo girl then whipping her until she bled. I was transformed into the nightmare of every housewife preparing dinner. I held up quite well, despite the scalding sun on outdoor shoots in Vassouras. Next to the velvety threads of the rich, my rural henchman's costume was a gift from the gods. And that's how I became ambivalent about my work. Who cared about the result, as long as I kept up with my lines and didn't trip on the furniture. I conflated having a profession with having a job. Dionysus never forgave me, and I paid, with Lear, the sins of those inglorious years.

At what point did I turn into a cynic? That is the question. I think that was the moment, whip in hand, laughing at what I'd made of myself. The truth is that I could no longer remember why I had chosen this profession.

WE WERE A HANDFUL of kids crammed into the back of a bus. Having recently graduated from diapers, we had drunk in the words of the Campos's lecture on theater and revolution. *We must make an art that serves the people*, insisted the professor, a performing-arts guru from the architecture department at the Universidade Federal do Rio de Janeiro. *I'm not talking about folklore, for fuck's sake! The Queen of the airwaves! This marginalization that favors a backward bourgeoisie*, he added, shrouded in certainties. I made a great effort to pay attention, sleep weighing down my eyelids and my back with a crick from so much road. I knew his speech by heart, but I was too young, too ignorant, to tell him to shut his trap. Campos had elevated repeating himself to an art form. I lied to my mother, saying I was going camping along the coast of Bahia, I grabbed my guitar, stuffed a change of clothes into my backpack, and headed for the bus station without any idea what fate had in store for me. It took us two days to make it to Recife and six more hours on a flatbed pickup before we reached the coastal plains of Pernambuco. The sun was skin-splitting when the Kombi belonging to the Party rolled up to get us outside of the tiny Xexéu church. A sketchy-looking dude stepped out from behind the wheel, opened the jammed door, and told us to get inside. Campos didn't let up even on this final stretch. *In Brazil*, he continued, *capital fed off a disgusting feudalism, an archaic paternalism*, as the driver nodded in agreement. As we rode on, cross-eyed from the distance and the never-ending refrain, I let my thoughts wander, admiring the sugarcane plantations that filled the dusty window with green.

Two years of Bolshevik indoctrination had brought me to that point.

Vanity was to blame. A fact that, at the time, I would have been hard-pressed to admit, but which today is clear. My stage presence and vocal gifts had earned me the role of Chief Seattle reading his letter to the President of the United States in an amateur production my first year of college. *The great chief in Washington wants to buy our lands . . .* there were ten uninterrupted minutes of applause and a line of girls eager to ingratiate themselves with the chief. *This is what I want from life*, I thought. We did political theater, with the actors on the front, standing at attention, vociferating our lines with our necks stretched skyward, as though facing an enormous wall. It was awful, but it was leftist. I would have settled for that, resting on my laurels, but Campos had other ambitions. The military had set fire to the headquarters of the National Student Union, the dictatorship tightened its grip, the trendy professors were removed from their positions; disobedience onstage wasn't enough, we had to resist, honor our status as card-carrying national heroes. We organized marches, ran from police, we sang the national anthem draped in the flag; we wept when José

Dirceu was thrown in jail in Ibiúna and when Gilberto Gil and
Caetano Veloso were forced into exile. When classes resumed,
Campos began his catechism. He started the semester speaking
of the conscientization of the masses and made clear his disdain
for the approbation of the submissive bourgeoisie. *The artist's
duty is not to work for the people but with the people*, he said, citing
Paulo Freire's successful literacy drive. *I have no use for a theater
about Grandpa spying Grandma's girly bits!* he bridled. *I want
students committed to the fight against this disgraceful conformism.*
He looked us in the eyes, like a guard dog sniffing out doubt.
I was a normal young man, I lived with my parents, I'd never
made my bed and had impressed my colleagues with my artistic
gifts, that was enough for me, but I was afraid to admit my
own submissiveness. I spent the year getting acquainted with
public improv, I did street theater, invisible theater, I idolized
Vianinha, Guarnieri, Boal; and I read, without understanding a word, Marx, Lenin, and Marcuse. So deep did Campos's
Cuban pretensions run that he branded the engagé Teatro de
Arena conservative and claimed the Cinema Novo had been
co-opted. In October, our guide proposed a summer camp in
the Northeastern backlands. We were to have two months of
rehearsals, we'd spend Christmas with family, and then set off
for the unknown. Some signed on right away, others traded
tense glances, but no one had the guts to say they weren't going.
We considered putting on a rural version of *They Don't Wear
Black Tie*, but Campos was of the opinion that trade unionism
and agrarian reform didn't mix. We chose Brecht instead.
We adapted the system of master–servant relations in *Mr.*

Puntila and His Man Matti to a sugarcane plantation. Then it was workshop after workshop, and here's a show of power for you, one group giving the other a thrashing. My stature and pedigree took me out of the running for a role as one of the beleaguered, I was accustomed to dealing more blows than I received. The poor wretches suffered a great deal, but in the end they turned the tables, raining down on the dominant classes. Campos harbored a healthy aversion to all forms of authority, except for his own, and decided to scrap the protagonist. I balked because I'd won the post of prima donna after my success as Chief Seattle. I masked my disappointment and feigned acceptance of the democratic proposal. A scepter was placed in the middle of a circle to be passed from cast member to cast member—whoever wielded the thing would be Mr. Puntila. The idea worked when there was no audience, but as soon as a few friends showed up an all-out battle for the object ensued. We suspended the performance for a group mea culpa. Theory was one thing, practice was another. We persisted two more weeks until Campos invited an acquaintance of his to assess the work. This acquaintance was an insipid actor but respected on the frontlines of the artistic resistance to the military dictatorship, he'd been part of the Nara Leão musical *Opinion* and was part of the People's Culture Center. Distraught at his students' poor performance, Campos discreetly rose to his feet and whispered in my ear that I was not to surrender the scepter under any circumstances. My six feet and velvet vocal chords, once again, guaranteed me the choice role. *Puntila soy yo*, I screamed in the bathroom, washing my hands after a taking a victory piss. Not so much in service to the revolution but to cement my place as the troupe's lead actor, I agreed to participate when they forced an extra run at the Teatro Municipal do Crato. You can abolish class, distribute the wealth, but no one's yet invented the formula for ending narcissism.

Even today, after years and years, I can see that the casting never escapes the eternal rules of the *physique du role*. Some were born to be the heartthrob, others the virtuous father. Others the tyrant, others the court jester. Most came into the world to be extras.

†

The Kombi dropped us off at a two-room *bajareque* hut made of wattle and daub, a collection of kissing bugs generously given shelter in the cracks in the walls. The bathroom was a hole surrounded by clapboard behind the house, situated next to the wood-burning stove covered by a roof of broken tiles. Campos took the bedroom for himself and we were left the living room. Grateful for having made it alive, and invested in our patriotic revolutionary mission, we dumped our crap on the dirt floor and scurried outside to make contact with the area's cold-lunchers. Their local association was closed. It was after noon and folks had got up early to cut sugarcane on the neighboring farms. Disappointed, we shuffled back to the crumbling hut to relax. Those without sleeping bags dozed piled up in hammocks. I was startled awake, drooling, unsure where I was. I nudged my colleague sharing the hammock with me, we shook the rest awake, but our haste was for naught. Eleven-fifteen at night, the city had already gone to bed. We lit a fire in front of the hut, put up with Campos and his theories until he tired of the sound of his own voice, sang some of Geraldo Vandré's hits, and missed the sunrise. There was a clear disconnect between the hours of the people and those of our militant vanguard. When, finally, we synced our schedules, Campos's lips opened in an angelic smile, a silly expression I'd never seen cross his face before, and he reverently approached one of the locals. A tiny man, he could have been thirty or eighty years old, it was impossible to tell. With his skin made leather by the sun, his enormous shovel-hands, and a half-dozen teeth, he looked like a totem pole, solid, sturdy like the trunk of an Ipê, and he looked directly at those he was addressing. Campos extended his soft hand, which dissolved in the stubby man's firm handshake. The Kombi driver gave the sign for the comrades to introduce ourselves. We waved politely, while they removed their hats in a sign of respect. I expressed my surprise at their leather coverings in the abrasive heat and was told that the armor protected them from the sugarcane fibers, sharp as a razor. Proud of the impact of this explanation, a few removed their coats to display their scars. Curiosity broke the ice. As I admired the marred skin, I sensed that a frou-frou like me, fine flower of Rio's crème de la crème, had nothing to offer to these wild creatures. I was a malnourished animal, wanting of melanin, calluses, brawn, decency. *We're sailing on a leaky ship*, I thought, when the Kombi driver informed them that we'd be giving a performance Sunday afternoon. The laborers had no reaction, put their hats back on their heads, begged our pardon, and climbed aboard a rig for another day of exploitation. Campos watched, moved, as the truck pulled away down the dirt road and decreed that, one day, we would possess the maturity to understand the meaning behind what had just happened there. He grabbed a fistful of dirt, swearing like Scarlett O'Hara that he would not rest until he had seen the end of all social injustice in the country. I had my doubts about his oath. The episode awakened an adverse feeling inside, a feeling that the rube before me, thick as a tree trunk, possessed much greater clarity about the meaning of life than our Soviet mentor. My doubts notwithstanding, I joined in the chorus of applause. The driver ended the formalities and ordered us to form a circle and extend the tarp across the empty lot between the houses. That was where we would have our meetings and rehearsals, the cradle of Rio's university contingent of Che Guevara's socialist uprising.

The days passed calmly. We rehearsed in the afternoons, we took refreshing baths in the pond with the children in the morning, we ate goat and ground tapioca with the married women. A few of the girls made eyes at us, but the driver warned that questions of honor in that place were resolved at knifepoint. *Better to mount a horse*, he laughed, *if none of you know how, I can show you*. Everyone got the message. On Sunday, the village threw a party to celebrate our performance. The audience came freshly showered, carrying rock candy, cheese, flour, and cachaça. The couples arm in arm, the girls seductive, the children scampering like swallows between their parents' legs. A beautiful thing, I must say.

Ladies and gentlemen, we present today
A prehistoric animal—the landowner
In simpler language: an agrarian proprietor
You know the citizen well.

The opening of *Mr. Puntila*. Despite my ideological misgivings, taking the stage restored my faith in humanity, a genuine concern for the misadventures of man. I hadn't yet discovered cynicism. When we finished, the men's indifference to Brecht and the women's disappointment in the lack of romance were unmistakable. Yet our little escapade had its purpose. Next, we started a pickup soccer game before gathering around a guitar. They pulled out their violas and that's when we found communion that had nothing to do with doctrine. Indelible revelry, sincere joy, brotherly love, art; something that had nothing to do with our activist mentor's discourse. Where Campos saw marginalization, I felt a sensual interaction, connected to the senses, far removed from everything I'd committed myself to doing there. The experience created lasting ties between us and the community. The women agreed to join in the chorus and the men participated in the workshops. We spent a week preparing for the next meeting, working on short improv scenes around the land issue. Campos didn't stray from his playbook, his way of seeing the world top-down, in a benevolent dictatorship that aroused my suspicions.

When the long-awaited Sunday afternoon arrived, the serfs again showed up smelling of soap and huddled beneath the tarp. The director called for a volunteer to join the game.

The people laughed, excited and sheepish, egging each other on to see who had the courage. The least suspicious among them took one step forward as the others roared. I was summoned. We stood facing one another. *What might your name be?* Campos asked him with all the polish of a backwoods variety show host. *Jorge Araújo*, the man responded. Applause. *So tell me, Mr. Araújo, who is the most powerful man you've ever met, sir? Cavalcanti*, the young man said without blinking. *Well, sir, I want you to pretend that Mario here, Mr. Araújo, is master Cavalcanti.* A gawky smile opened across the poor guy's face as he realized how ridiculous it was for two grown men to play make-believe. I didn't return his gentle expression. Holding up my end, I stared him down and attacked, informing him that from that day on the work week would run from Sunday to Sunday, with no days off. The audience laughed in recognition of this incarnation of the devil. *The farm has to turn a profit and I can't pay some loafer like you, sir, to chit-chat!* I concluded in a rage. The man started timidly and Campos interceded, keeping the tension taut. *Is this right?* he asked those present, and we heard a resounding *No*. *Does he share the profits he reaps with you, Mr. Araújo?* Campos continued, and the boy, saying nothing, shook his head. *And do you think it's right to work from sunup to sundown to make money for the man who owns these lands, sir?* the professor went on. Araújo registered an audible *No*. *Say it again, big guy!* I challenged him. *No, it's not right*, he responded with conviction. *Well, sir, know that you stand before a Cavalcanti, and no Cavalcanti came into the world to be told No by some mud-footed peon*, I dialed in, three decibels higher than expected. The blood drained from Araújo's face. A solitary boo resounded across the audience. *Which one of you was the big man?* came my violent response. Everyone retreated in heavy silence. I followed up with some comic relief. I leapt across the stage, somewhere between powerful and pathetic, repeating that my business was profit, moola, cash money, and I pretended to swallow a few coins to the delight of the young children. The tension tempered, I assumed once again the virulence of the soulless master. *Vacation time is over, you understand? And I want to see if there's a macho among you, with the balls to stand up to a Cavalcanti!* I provoked. The kids all started to scream, the boos became a chorus, hysteria reigned. Campos gave the sign for the group to form a circle around me. Protected by mercenaries wielding broomsticks, I continued where I'd left off, mimicking a coward in a medieval pantomime. The jamboree reached its apex. The pip-squeaks started throwing dirt, the old folks began cursing, and Araújo asserted his valor once again, sticking his finger in my face. This was the uprising. We wrapped the scene triumphant, we applauded and were applauded. Campos narrowly escaped a heart attack.

At night, in the heat of the firepit inside the hut that we had already taken to calling home, he was suddenly possessed with the spirit of Antônio Conselheiro. Our professor couldn't stop philosophizing, drawing out new strategies and making calculations. *In two years, not even, look at Cuba!* he shouted, *ours will be a socialist country.* We considered the possibility and went to sleep swaddled in that illusion.

The light mood of that afternoon vanished in the coming weeks. Sundays were dedicated to testimony about the injustices visited upon the laborers. We collected hair-raising details, murders and bloodbaths, gang rapes and slave labor, and we set aside the most emblematic cases to set for the stage. Not everyone took up the routine, but six of the workers were diligent attendees. One of them clearly suffered some mental disturbance. Unable to parse fact from fiction, he had a conniption each time the indignation rose to his head.

One fateful Sunday, Campos sent me and my broomstick-wielding thugs to one side and huddled, on the extreme opposite side of the tarp, with ten peasants who had shown up for the experiment. I sat perched in a high-backed chair, the throne of the much feared Cavalcanti, who'd been promoted to a permanent fixture in our little jaunts. In a conspiratorial tone, Campos asked the ten men, all of them with Indian blood, to have a good look at that son of a harlot rocking back and forth on his throne. *This is the guy who exploits you*, he said, *who makes a living off of your work, who takes advantage of your poverty*. Those who attended regularly were already familiar with the make-believe routine, but the four new guys, plus the schizo, convinced themselves, though Campos didn't notice, that he was telling the truth. *Now I want you to go over there, right up next to him, and unload everything you've been through right on his neck*. The group prepared to walk in a block, while the nutjob, trailed by the four newbies, took the lead, and then they went berserk. My fictitious guard turned white when he saw the ferocious platoon and fled, leaving my Cavalcanti entirely unprotected. I had no time to react. The madman dragged me by the nape of my neck and threw me to the ground, and the others rained down upon me. I, who had never known a beating, was now taking a thrashing from five fist-flinging savages. *This is it*, I thought. I defended myself as best I could while shouting IT'S THEATER! IT'S JUST THEATER! My friends ran to my aid, four of them retreated, Campos gave the order to suspend the game, but the maniac only slowed down after being surrounded. His mother was fetched to look after the wild bull. She came in alarm, repeating her son's name until he calmed down. They embraced and the lunatic began weeping convulsively. We watched as he retreated with his tail between his legs. Before stepping away from the tarp, his mother delivered some harsh words.

"Don't any of you have a heart? Using my son like this. Can't you see he doesn't understand? That no one understands what you came here to do?"

We fell silent. Campos decided the performance had come to an end. I wiped away the blood, my executioners apologized, and I told them they had nothing to apologize for. We decided to keep those who could grasp metaphors, we sent the rest away, and we went back home hanging our heads.

That evening, there was no fire.

The incident provoked a change in the plan set forth by Campos, who abandoned the amateur circus to focus on the conscientization of the masses. The tarp became a classroom. Before I knew it, there Campos was convincing five peons to take up arms. I think it must have been the isolation, the half-truths repeated a thousand times over, who knows. I don't know at exactly which moment this shift took place. From one moment to the next, we started taking target practice with some rusty revolvers supplied by the Kombi driver. He had connections to the army, I think he must have gone clandestine, but given that he always seemed on edge and seldom spoke, no one had the audacity to ask him. We replaced our usual warm-up with a military routine. We ran with rocks hoisted, we crossed streams, we underwent endurance tests. Campos continued overseeing the theory classes, but the chauffeur took over the practical matters. I thought about running away, but I opted for prudence. Sergeant Six-Cylinder filled me with dread. Without realizing, we'd become hostage to him. There were only two weeks left until the beginning of the school year, I thought, Campos isn't crazy enough to give up university to involve himself in some fiasco in the Pernambuco wilderness. To calm everyone's nerves, he arrived one day with a copy of *The Petty Bourgeois*, saying we'd do a staging on our return. Our return. The word filled us with hope. We read Gorki before bed, fully aware that the theater had been relegated to the background. The man dealing the cards now was the transportation director.

We were all sleeping heavily when we heard a pounding on the door. We jumped out of bed, I remember the most radicalized one of us carrying a revolver and lying in wait behind the door. *This whole thing's got out of control*, I thought. The pounding continued. It was the boss, the Kombi driver, ordering us to open up. Campos came from the bedroom with a gun stuffed in his pants and opened the latch. The driver stepped in with the same five guys as always, locked us all inside, and ordered us to snuff out the candles. Something awful was about to happen. I thought of my mother, of how I missed Rio and its coastline, the Lagoa, the girls on the beach, the music, the beauty, and the sea.

Araújo, with whom I'd shared the spotlight during the glory days of our improv sketches, asked for our attention and explained, excitedly, all the trouble. Cavalcanti's thugs had kidnapped his brother, on account of the fantasies he'd put into the heads of the farmworkers. In the beginning, it was just a threat, but his brother refused to listen and insisted on catechizing the other men. That night, four armed men had burst into the house, where the guy lived with his wife and four small children, and dragged him outside to teach the entire village a lesson. Bloodied but with a short fuse, he kept repeating out loud, for anyone to hear, what he'd learned from Campos about the revolution. They hit him harder, but there wasn't a prayer that could make him quiet. They even fired their guns but, confused by his rambling, they thought it prudent to take him to the colonel. *That's where he is now*, said the Kombi driver, *they must have squeezed him. By now, he must have told them everything he knows. They might come seize our arms*, he barked, *the hour has come. We're gonna bring your brother home alive*, he promised, placing his hand on the shoulder of my former stage mate.

We turned to Campos. We couldn't believe it. This wasn't part of the summer camp we'd signed up for. He immediately recognized the contradiction. He was a theater professor, he lacked the skills to lead a suicide mission. At the moment it mattered most, his words failed him. We stood there, waiting for our leader to explain that we were architecture students, amateur artists, momma's boys, innocent virgins! Any excuse to make the man back off his call to arms. The man built like a tree trunk, the one who had welcomed us at the very beginning, understood our hesitation and drew his machete. We recoiled in unison and he spat on the floor, making his disappointment clear. *You fill us with ideas*, he began, offended, *but when the hour of need arrives, you don't want to dirty your pretty little hands. If no one here is man enough, I am*, he proclaimed with a scowl, and he stormed outside, trailed by Araújo and the rest. The darkness swallowed the last of them. The man from the Kombi stood there one more second, his gaze shooting right through Campos. Before following the troops, he warned that, upon his return, he was going to have a serious conversation with the group.

The professor waited until he could be certain they were far away. We listened to their voices growing more distant until only the crickets remained. *What are you waiting for?* the director asked, *grab what you can and let's go. Hurry!* he ordered. We grabbed what we could and dashed through the clearing. It was a moonless night. We struggled through the shadows, looking for a path that would lead us away from that place. We fled on foot, we didn't dare mutter a word. We had raised the ire of Cavalcanti and those in his employ, we ran the risk of falling victim to an ambush, of ending up in jail, of being tortured, killed, victims of revenge. We faced imminent danger the entire way from Xecú to Palmares. Those were twenty-three kilometers of perseverance. When the sun rose, we caught sight of the *quilombo* of Zumbi; from there, we took a bus to Recife and then another back to Rio de Janeiro.

†

I wept as Christ came into view.

I held my mother in my arms. She stared at my beard, the bruises, she wanted to know what had gone wrong in Bahia. I changed the subject, telling her I was tired, and I announced my plans to quit architecture school and become an actor.

My mother was alarmed but thought it better to put the conversation off for another day.

I buried the armed resistance, my militancy, I burned my photographs of Che, I threw Marx, Marcuse, and Brecht in the trash. The world was an awful place, but I didn't want anything more to do with it. Cowardice? So be it.

AUNT NEUSA and my cousins would horrify old Campos. The people he was always talking about only existed in Canudos, in the backlands of Guimarães Rosa, or in the sprawling ABC industrial region. Tijuca was not part of the audience he envisioned. Mirror images of the dysfunctional characters in a Nelson Rodrigues play, my relatives would surely face the firing squad in my old master's El Dorado.

I, who had given up arms to combat the sea of troubles and put an end to them, preferred to sleep, and perhaps dream of a theater that would shock the Praça Sáenz Peña.

Pressured by my family to finish school, I deferred for a year but didn't drop out. If I were arrested one day, my mother counseled, my diploma would guarantee my right to a special cell. It was one reason—a very good one—not to tell the administrators at UFRJ to go to hell. Still a student and free of my obligation to tackle the country's social inequality, I dedicated myself to youth's more mundane pleasures. After class, I would relax amid the waves near the pier, play soccer on the beach with the similarly disengaged, seduce the girls in their thongs, and join those applauding the sunset over Leblon. Musicians, actors, filmmakers, and intellectuals visited

68

the thin strip of sand. The sun was witness to how much I idolized them.

Two adult hippies, half-bald, half-hairy, made an impression in the midst of such varied fauna. Owners of the Teatro Ipanema, Rubens Corrêa and Ivan de Albuquerque recalled rock and roll druids and had broken from the radicalism then in vogue. Curious, and still covered in sea salt, I walked two blocks along the street running parallel to the wavy beach promenade and stopped in front of the apartment building that housed a show venue in the basement. I bought a ticket for *Hair*.

I was never the same again.

Seated in row J, I was overcome by a raging desire, a spontaneous joy, which I never knew existed. These people screw, a lot, I thought, agog at the visual orgy of the denim-toting tribe. I had learned from Campos that I'd been born in an underdeveloped country, sad, condemned to backwardness, whose awakening would only come through a bloody civil war. The people in the theater that day completely destroyed that belief.

At the height of my epiphany, my eyes locked with those of a nude brunette with disheveled hair and perfect tits. She marched forward in line with some more shaggy-haired people then struck a pose before an open-mouthed audience for the long minute permitted by government censors. I went nuts. I jerked off all night thinking about Sônia Braga. A wild goddess, an Aphrodite of the same pantheon to which Leila and Gal Costa belonged. I waited at the exit to see them up close. Armando Bógus, the absolute ruler of the place, walked out arm in arm with Sônia. They were dating. Leaning up against a lamppost, I longed to be one of them, to be him, Bógus. And I would be, a decade after that evening.

Overcome with excitement, I skipped class the next day and stood vigil at the door of the Ipanema. I bought tickets to all the performances that week. I did the same thing the following week and soon became close to the girl selling tickets. Thanks to her, I learned that the director had opened auditions for replacements for two actors in the chorus. They were looking for hirsute young men who could command the stage, one's mane being as important or more so than one's artistic gifts. I grabbed my friend Jackson Five from the beach, with his black power that would have them lining up on the sidewalk, and we headed for the Teatro Jovem in Botafogo. A long line extended out and around the front door. Jackson shined during the singing test, imitating Michael singing *ABC*; I didn't do bad myself in the voice test, declaiming the old letter of the Indian Seattle. To our shock, we passed. *We did it, man, we did it!* I said over and over again to Jackson, my eyes filled with tears, as I squeezed his Afro between my hands. They invited us back the following Thursday. There was no rehearsal, no preparation. They set us loose, waltzing down the aisle on the lower level amid all the lunatics. Sônia here, Sônia there, weed, ass, tits, laughs, total gratification. We climbed the stairs toward the stage. Before I realized it, I was naked, standing next to Jackson, at a respectable distance from Bógus's backside, but vying to brush up against that of the tigress Sônia.

I decided to abandon architecture once and for all and moved out of my parents' house to share a two-bedroom apartment in Laranjeiras with Jackson and a couple of musician friends. My father cut my allowance. Maria Amélia helped me on the sly, though she suffered from her son's wild streak. We were so poor that we wrote our names on each piece of cheese or cup of yogurt we put in the fridge. The couple had the habit of spitting on whatever they bought to keep Jackson and me away.

With a foot in the door at the Ipanema, we were welcomed to the cast of *Time to Rock and Roll*. We passed out bread during the opening as though it were the sacred host, and we dropped acid in order to elevate us to a holy state. Our success made history. At the last performance it was so packed that there was no room for us to perform. Rubens took the caravan to the beach, marching down Rua Joana Angélica, and we found ourselves in the sand, in the open air, before multitudes of devoted fans. I became mystic, cosmic, one with the earth.

Campos would have had me taken out and shot if he'd seen that. Aunt Neusa wouldn't have recognized me. Just as she didn't recognize me on the afternoon that the Paulo de Frontin overpass came down as I was visiting my grandmother. Silence came over the family as they watched me come in through the kitchen, they thought I was a burglar. I explained that I was doing a hippie play and my aunt let out a sympathetic sigh, promising to say an Our Father to change my luck. I thanked her without engaging. We watched the news reports about the accident, but they didn't pay attention, they were all worked up because the neighbor girl was going to marry. Aunt Neusa had nurtured the illusion that she would be a good match for me. Perhaps in hopes of consoling me for my dwindling marriage prospects, my aunt confided that the neighbor girl was no longer a virgin, she had undergone a reconstructive hymen surgery to keep her misstep from her future husband. My god, what was the world coming to? I had spent the night with two fans of *Time to Rock and Roll*, one of them Jackson's girlfriend, I almost confessed, but I didn't want to shock my aunt. I limited myself to feigning surprise, drinking a strong cup of coffee, and grabbing the first bus back to Shangri-La.

My plans to stick around at the Ipanema went down the drain the day that Rubens and Ivan announced the decision to found a community in the countryside. Together, they were running away to a forest reserve in the lowlands of Friburgo, with the aim of finding refuge in dark times. Vaccinated by my previous misadventure, I preferred to remain cityside.

THE LANDING GEAR pounded against the runway. My memories of the Ipanema vanished with the jolt, run off by my routine concern that the pilot might forget to hit the brakes. Congonhas is not an airport, it's an aberration carved into the heart of South America's most populous city. From the window, during landing, it's possible to see the clothes hung on the verandas of the thousands of homes that surround the end of the runway. The number of fools living there only multiplied, clinging to the low statistical probability of exploding in a disaster. The short runway ends abruptly, in a steep hill that runs along the expressway. To avoid any tragedies, it's necessary to reverse the turbines full speed at landing. In July 2007, the pilot of TAM flight 3054 accelerated by mistake, flew straight over the cars, and blew up the plane on the other side of the avenue. I followed the calamity on the television, just as I'd done when the Paulo de Frontin collapsed. Terrified at the thought of taking a flight the next day, I drove for six long hours along the Dutra expressway to fulfill my part in the run of *Right You Are (If You Think So)* at the Teatro Cultura Artística, later consumed in a colossal fire.

We taxied forever. The day had begun badly. I stood waiting
for an eternity, along with the rest of the passengers crammed
into the aisle between seats, waiting on the terminal shuttle
bus. From there, I would head off to bury *Lear*'s mortal remains.

São Paulo smells awful. It's something those who live there
don't notice. The shortest time away, however, sharpens one's
critical olfactories. Every time I return to the city, I'm shocked at
the concentration of exhaust, lead, and methane accumulated
in the atmosphere. Especially between April and June, when
the dry weather causes the mineral particles to glimmer in the
air. That day was no different. At the intersection of Avenida
Paulista and Rua da Consolação, the air quality meter read POOR.

†

Milena gnawed her nails at a table in the café of the famed hotel
that had accepted our barter. I avoided her. I approached the
reception desk, closed out the accounts without checking the
bills, was kind enough to pay for the extra expenses incurred
by the team, gave a nice fat tip to the receptionist, and asked
them to release the impounded luggage. My intention was to
take care of all outstanding details in time to grab the next
flight back. I wanted to avoid another anxiety attack from Maria
Amélia; the previous night, it had been terrible to see her doped
up at the hospital. The producer saw things were moving along
and came to help. *Everything's paid*, I said, aware that I would
have to tighten my belt. I lit another cigarette, the fifth of the
day, while she verified with the driver of the van-for-hire the
addresses of those who were waiting for their belongings to

be returned. I ordered a double espresso and sat down at the bar. *It's better we take our meeting somewhere else*, the producer advised. *I can't handle another stop*, I snapped. *Paulo slept in the hotel, drank too much last night, and missed his meeting at the TV station, I don't want to be here when he wakes up*, she warned. I shot back the espresso and offered her my chair, without giving her room for negotiation. With deep dark circles under her eyes, Milena obeyed, opened her luggage, and dumped a pile of receipts on the table to speed things along.

The cast had gone home the day before. Lineu began having heart palpitations and had to be hospitalized. The health insurance would cover the costs. *That's the only good news I have to give you*, Milena told me. *Other than that, I've just received a message that the accounting report for our run in Rio was rejected by the Ministry of Culture*. They had suspected us of issuing phony receipts, they took a fine-tooth comb to things. I asked about the report from Gomes, the accountant. She responded that she'd left him endless messages but hadn't yet received any response. She lowered her head, half-ashamed, half-glum. I had my suspicions. *The asshole pockets 10 percent of the whole joke and I'm the one who gets screwed*, I thought. Right, of course.

I riffled through the papers, the bureaucratic labyrinth of laws governing support for the arts, longing for the days when theater productions operated on the modest scale of a corner grocer. The box office opened, the tickets were counted, the money stuffed in a safe and taken under one's arm to the nearest bank. Everything in cash, no bad checks. Accounts were tallied on a paper sack, simple arithmetic, adding and subtracting. Actors and stagehands signed any old receipt and it was all taken care of. The Jurassic Gomes had been with me since that time. I'd met him in a tinderbox theater during a run of *A Razor to the Flesh*. He helped run the show and had alerted me to the need to declare my earnings. I laughed at his advice. I considered myself an aspiring actor, an amateur talent, and I thought it was ridiculous to be thrown together in the same category of the so-called independent professionals who clock in and have taxes docked from their pay stubs. I viewed the theater as something on the fringes, immured against bureaucracy. Over the years, however, with my increased earnings, the cost of living, the plays I produced made for some complicated financial arrangements and Gomes was suddenly an éminence grise, my constant shadow, who handled, in his own way, the legal side of my daily life.

Together we prospered. The musty room where he had his office, on the eighth story of an old building in downtown Rio, soon expanded until it took up half the floor. Of the twenty doors lining the dark hallway, each smelling like a crematorium, eleven belonged to him. Gomes commanded an army of merciless expediting agents, aces at cutting lines, taking care of the necessary seals with shady notary publics, and doctoring earnings. Unlike the hungry lion of Brasilia, Gomes thought it was obscene to pay taxes on a full house. It proved, for X, Y, and Z reasons, impossible to both satiate the tax authorities and keep a show onstage. In cahoots with the theaters, he doctored the bordereaux, always reporting only half the ticket sales. He honored everyone's percentage and salary to the cent. He knew he depended on the silence of those involved to keep the pirate ship afloat. What more could one want? I saw myself as a moral safeguard, a reflection of the human comedy, freedom of expression embodied. Art was above that sort of rapaciousness. I had come up as an actor during a brutal dictatorship, wooed by the idea that cheating on my taxes was a form of resistance. *Don't show me any spreadsheets, or I'll lose my voice!* I joked, and Gomes nearly fell down laughing. My refusal to deal with the national treasury satisfied his ambitions for power. *Mario, querido, I guarantee it!* he would parry, and I slept the sleep of the innocent, concentrating on the vicissitudes of character.

As the country's twenty-five-year dictatorship was winding down, the persecution of artists came to an end, and almost in recompense for the dark years, new mechanisms of cultural funding came into vogue. Instead of the parrots at the bank, we were soon dealing with the marketing departments of large corporations interested in sponsoring the arts, and Gomes swiftly reached new heights. He quit being the disgusting slob who wore polyester pants and patent-leather shoes. He bought a suit, an ugly one but a suit nonetheless, and redid one of the rooms of his office, the first one, which he kept for himself, almost out of superstition. He painted the walls a salmon color, redid the sofa in purple Nappa leather; hired a young secretary and stuck her in a windowless cubicle near the entrance, behind a Formica divider. The swashbuckling dispatchers he put along the remaining hallway bays, where they could speak with the boss's new office through a new internal phone network, bought at its weight in gold, together with a dedicated air-conditioning system. At the door to room 801, a gold-plated plaque read: GOMES ACCOUNTING LTDA—PRESIDENT'S OFFICE. Crowing over his prodigious ascension, he began to mediate transactions between the producers and the firms participating as sponsors. Gomes took classes, specializing in the area of law that governed the new forms of financing, and his importance grew, along with the percentage he charged to impose order on the chaos. It was no different with *Lear*.

I met Milena Jovic thanks to him, a young producer whom Gomes had worked with on a production of *Aida* at the Teatro Municipal. I didn't hesitate to accept his suggestion. Milena had a red-hot contact inside an engineering firm, and she'd come off quite well commanding backstage operations at the opera. Stein's ambitions had been as great as Verdi's, mine no less modest. Confident in my financial advisors and his "I guarantee it!" I closed my eyes, as was my habit, and we signed an agreement.

†

Now, Milena was looking at me completely spent; Gomes had vanished and the taxman, for the first time in decades, was aware of my existence.

Two years earlier, I had walked at her side, filled with hope, through the hallways of the headquarters of the firm that had signed on as a patron of the arts. It was my chance to land the project that would tear me out of my decade-long professional slump.

I'd spent the weekend with Stein in Corrêas, where I formalized my invitation for him to return to the theater as director. There, we drank in front of the fire and agreed on all the details, especially on the need to recover the precepts we considered inseparable from the stage: honesty and audacity. We spoke ill of all our colleagues who had other productions, we recognized our own lack of ambition at times, and we reiterated the importance of revisiting *Lear*, the best translation of our own experience, two dethroned kings, lost in the desert of ideas that was contemporary mediocrity. I felt an energy the entire drive down the sierra, I could already see the blessed future.

The secretary to the firm's marketing director, Milena's cousin, confirmed the company's interest on Monday morning, we'd been bumped ahead of five other projects. We set up a meeting for Tuesday.

†

Mota Filho was an elegant man. Elegantly slim. Sporting a fresh tan, a manicure, and taut skin thanks to exfoliant creams, he professed to be a lover of the highest culture. On the wall behind the Italian chair where he sat up straight, Mota displayed the side of the bus belonging to Raymundo Colares, a leading figure of the '60s generation of Brazilian artists. *I have Ligia, I've got Helio, I've got Cildo, Guignard, and a Tarsila known to few, but I'm too envious to show them*, he confided. We'd barely sat down before he started talking, jumping from one subject to another, citing books, films, renowned directors, at the same time he performed the honors as host. Belching erudition was the guy's favorite pastime. A compulsive man,

79

he recited Whitman, declaimed Bandeira, and spat out whole passages of Shakespeare by heart, and in the original. *Life's but a walking shadow. . . .* We patiently endured this show, waiting for him to, at some point, deign to speak to us. *Why not* Macbeth?! *The problem is the Portuguese, who would translate it?* he answered his own question without taking a breath. Lear? I jumped at the cue, interrupting his soliloquy. *Yes, it's* Lear, *isn't it?* he answered, *who translated? Millôr,* I told him, and he nodded approvingly, he could think of no one better. *And the Fool?* He paused. *The fool . . . ?* I asked, not understanding that casting decisions had entered the picture. I mentioned Arlindo, but he didn't bother listening, his focus had turned to bragging how, when still very young, he'd watched the production by the National Theater, with Anthony Hopkins in the role of the king. And as though he were intimate with the star, he asserted that the unpleasant experience had caused him to give up on England and deliver himself to the well-paid conformism of Hollywood. Then he paraded through the hall of historic productions he'd seen during the ten years he'd lived in London. Redgrave, Dench, McKellen, O'Toole. Joking, he advised me to find a mediocre actor to play the Fool—he'd actually used the English word, *fool*—returning to the Fool, whom he'd abandoned at some point in the lecture. *They steal the show, Mario, careful!* I should have listened to Mota. He explained that, were it up to him, he'd pour the entire budget into the project, but he'd need the board's approval. *No one likes Shakespeare!* he decreed with disdain, predicting the tribunal's criticism, and he immediately rebutted that in order to define what sort of art people like, you first had to define what sort of art they don't like. *Beethoven? Mahler? Brahms?!* he asked, addressing the ceiling as though consulting God. Then he rattled off all the unforgettable concerts he'd attended throughout his life, a sick Karajan conducting Strauss, confined to the lectern as he directed *Death and Transfiguration* to the very end. *What a Lear, though, Mario! What a Lear!* Humiliated, I felt like giving up. I was no Hopkins, nor McKellen, much less O'Toole; I wasn't at the level of any of the theatrical royalty he'd cited. I would leave that office several inches shorter than when I'd entered. *This man must have a clone at home*, I thought, to both hold down a job and have so many cultural experiences. Milena kept quiet; from the names he'd rattled off, she knew only Hopkins, and only because of the movie cannibal. I pretended to know more than she did, putting on my best poker face. Following this preamble, the conversation turned to numbers. Mota didn't flinch at the amount and even predicted an increase for the run in São Paulo. The firm would be celebrating its fiftieth anniversary the following year. *Why not have a reception on opening night?* he suggested creatively. I nearly knelt down at the unicorn's feet. We agreed to send the updated numbers, we exchanged handshakes, and he promised to be in touch soon to iron out the details.

Mota was there at the firm's fiftieth anniversary celebration, at the opening of the failed *Lear* run in São Paulo. He emitted a sharp whistle as he snored in his seat in the fifth row, next to his bleach-blonde wife. On her way out, Ana Claudia praised the costumes, though she found the play a bit depressing. Mota congratulated me for my courage, we took a selfie, and that was the last time I saw him.

†

Sitting in the hotel lobby, I suspected that the marketing director's affectation had some relation to Gomes's disappearance and Milena's disheartened expression. Absorbed in paranoid speculation, I extended my hand to the producer, in an attempt to relay a sense of calm. That's when I was thrust to the floor. Stunned, I turned to find myself face to face with Paulo. Milena was right, we should have avoided the hotel that morning. Mad as hell, the young heartthrob raised his fists, shouting that he had slept in that shithole just to have the satisfaction of breaking my face in. Milena tried to hold him back, but he threw her against the wall while the receptionist called security. I grabbed a chair for protection, Paulo kicked at me and my shield, I grabbed him around the midsection, protecting my face in the beast's armpit. We twirled down the hall like a couple in love. We fell on the couch, me on the bottom, him on top. The last thing I remember is Paulo's fist pulling back toward the ceiling before coming in toward my left eye.

Knockout.

BLACKING OUT had relieved my tension, I opened my functioning eyelid in the hospital where I'd slept the entire night, sprawled on the sofa next to Lineu's bed. Milena had set me up in the room, as Lineu's visitor. It wasn't long before my misfortunes multiplied, putting an end to my reprieve. A physical and moral pain, more moral than physical, too much to deal with. I wept. Lineu looked on in silence, offered me the glass of water resting on the nightstand, it was all he had to offer, and kept his eyes glued to the television. I whimpered as long as I could, until I grew tired. No one was coming to console me. I wiped my drool on the pillow and turned toward the TV on the wall. It was a biblical soap. *Is this what you've been watching?* I asked, intrigued. *I received a call to play a Hebrew elder*, my colleague explained, *I was going to refuse, but now that* Lear's *ended, I didn't have a choice*. Onscreen, an Egyptian soldier, wearing a skirt made of synthetic leather, seduced a virtuous slave girl. *I would make a good Roman*, I thought, *or a dastardly Pharaoh*. I weighed my chances in the new market. Was it divine providence sending a message to a lost sheep like me? I lacked faith. Lineu seemed to guess what I was thinking and confessed that this job prospect had saved him from palpitations the day before.

83

It was God, he said, *it was God*. We followed the drama until the next commercial break. Chicken wings for $2.99 were offered between the subjection of the chosen people and the barbarity of the idol-worshippers. I pictured myself before Mount Sinai, dancing around the golden calf. I'd been worshipping the wrong god. A role in that soap would pay the bills, I surmised, with enough left over to make partial amends for my sins. *The Bible is like Janete Clair*, Lineu said, *it has a life of its own, there's no going wrong, I'm resigned to it*. We shared a laugh at our lack of options. I silently sketched out my plans. First, I would try to get something in a high-end show, and if that went badly, I'd tackle the Bible. I had debts to honor, my mother's treatment, it wasn't the most encouraging of situations.

I turned my back on the only viable entertainment industry in Brazil spouting hard-edged truths, I refused roles, broke contracts, saying I needed to reinvent myself. They were gracious in their reaction, but they'd blacklisted me as unreliable. During nearly two years away, the crisis that had hit the music business around the turn of the millennium turned toward other industries. Audiences had migrated to the Internet. The old feud over audience had been split between smaller domains where the public found their entertainment, padding their own egos. Blacks and whites, young and old, homos and heteros spent hours hearts aflame for people just like them. To gain influence, all one needed was to sit in front of the computer and blurt out the most outrageous nonsense. Forget cast, scenery, writers, producers, directors, forget it all. The PR agencies, the foundation of the old castle, now adulated no-name exhibitionists with billions of likes. An alien invasion that had abducted the old production chain of which I had been part. Hundreds of people had lost their jobs, once lifetime gigs, while I dreamed of being a sensation with my Shakespeare. My vanity was worth as much as everyone else's, or even less. Between *Lear* and *Machine Gun Funk*, *Machine Gun Funk* came out victorious. This was the record of what had occurred during my months of exile. Only the religious channels remained immune to the Antichrist, replete with dramas faithful to their doctrine, offering a world of order, where good opposed evil in easy-to-digest doses. Sunday services consisted of propaganda and tithes, tax-free contributions, kept the Television Kingdom of God alive. Hats off. *Is it hard to get a job there?* I asked playfully. *They're still in need of some Philistines*, Lineu responded in earnest. *Change the channel*, I begged. *Put the news on.*

World economic crisis, terrorism, missiles and mutant mosquitoes; hurricanes, melting ice caps, droughts, and floods; corruption, crimes, and murder. The fall of the Roman Empire. The Apocalypse, like they knew only in the Middle Ages. What did an actor matter in the midst of this historic collapse? I was a museum piece, I read the printed newspaper, used a landline, ate gluten, took antibiotics, and loved nineteenth-century novels. I was thankful I didn't have children, one fewer future to worry about.

As the newspaper report ended, Milena turned up, showered and presentable. She seemed serene. Gomes had called back and committed to presenting a report about the production's financial activity. *I guarantee it!* was the message he'd sent. Well aware of the worthlessness of my accountant's buffoonish self-confidence, I preferred to put off the problem. I, too, decided to take a bath and softened the bruise on my face with some makeup borrowed from Milena. I got on a plane back to Rio, the final flight of the night. Maria Amélia, the other half of my vale of tears, awaited her husband-child at the hospital.

SHE WAS CALM when she greeted me, her humors tempered by the medication. She had a scare when she saw my swollen eyelid and I lied, telling her a book had fallen from the shelf, landing square on my eyebrow. Her expression softened, she flashed a motherly smile and ran her fingers through my hair. It was impossible to hold back my tears. I was overcome by what life had done to me. I needed her so badly, the only person who, I knew, loved me unconditionally. *Be careful, my son.* Son. She called me son. She still remembered. *I'm tired, Mom.* It was so good to call her mother. She took my hand firmly in hers. *Who isn't?* she replied. I sat there for a moment, clutching onto what was left of her. I took advantage of her momentary lucidity to explain that something terrible had happened to her. I asked her if she recalled having walked naked into the sea. *Did I?* she asked. *You did,* I responded.

That was when Maria Amélia recounted a disturbing dream she'd had the night before the accident.

*   *   *

After dropping her youngest son off at school, she tried going home but couldn't remember her address. She walked through the Jardim Botânico, walked up the tiny street where we lived and, to her horror, our house was nowhere to be found. In its place, they'd built a small apartment complex, with aluminum framing and frosted glass. On the second-floor porch of our neighbors' house, a man with a bushy mustache appeared. He was a police detective who worked at a station that had never existed there. Maria Amélia asked about a house in the German style, with white walls and dark rafters, but the guy responded that the only house like that which existed was his and one other, at the end of the street, about to be razed. Confused, she confessed she was lost.

The detective offered to accompany her, they walked together, he sought clues, tried to help. He suggested they retrace the route to the school, but Maria Amélia no longer knew the way. The truth is that she wasn't even certain if she had a child anymore, she suspected she'd been married, had moved to Ipanema, or Copacabana, she couldn't be sure. A duplex penthouse with a view to the sea. There she lived with her husband, they had no children. He performed calculations on the dining room table, surrounded by a wall of exposed brick.

The man offered her a ride. She accepted. They drove down Avenida Nossa Senhora de Copacabana. Maria Amélia admired the businesses, the packed stories, she'd given anything to fall into the routine. The car pulled up at the entrance to a full parking garage. *This isn't my building*, she protested, but the doorman assured her it was. On edge, she prayed that her husband was upstairs, she could grab her son at school and life would return to normal. She took the busy elevator and stepped out into the empty hallway, surrounded by doors. A short young woman with wide hips came to greet her. In a somber tone, she informed her that Maria Amélia was dead.

"Dead?" she asked, surprised.

"Dead," the young woman answered. "Do you feel anything?"

"No, I can't feel a thing."

"You see? You don't feel anything because you're dead."

Dead? How, if she was standing there? The young woman walked off without saying goodbye and Maria Amélia thought it best to leave. In the elevator, two women were talking about the latest episode of a soap opera, they didn't care for the lead actress and were complaining about the series' missing love stories. Years ago, they were much better, they decided. She agreed, things were better before, with her son at school and her husband in the living room.

She left the building in a worse state than when she'd arrived.

The doorman didn't address her, a passerby didn't complain when she bumped into him. *So then*, she thought, *this is what it's like to die, amid the indifference of everyone else. Forget your son, forget your husband, forget the apartment that backs up to the sea*, she reflected. The sea. Maria Amélia crossed the street without looking, what harm could there be? She heard brakes screech, a sign that someone could still see her. When she made it to the seaside promenade, she took off her shoes and walked across the strip of sand. The surging sea broke on the surf line. She tore off her blouse, her skirt, her undergarments, and stood there, nude, feeling the humid wind across her skin. Drawn forward by the receding waters, she walked toward the cold sea. A huge wave, enormous, she said, crashed right over her head. She rolled, turned over, then turned again. Not a bit panicked. Submerged, she opened her eyes and admired the surface from below. *It will be nice to depart this way*, she thought. Focused on her final moments, she struggled as she felt a strong arm drag her upward. She tried to break free but was brought to the surface. Her body was stretched out on the edge of the sea, between passersby. The lifeguards launched straight into mouth-to-mouth resuscitation, pressing down on her chest with both palms spread wide. Curious passersby formed a circle around her. *So then, someone can still see me*, she noted, she existed once again. Tired, she closed her eyes and swam in the endless darkness.

*   *   *

I thought it was just a dream, she said when she'd finished her story. I was speechless. During the last few days, I had treated her like some incapable child who needed to be fawned over like a little doll. Now I was discovering that, behind her blank expression, Maria Amélia was confronting the foreshadowing of her death, the abyss. Samuel Beckett. A writer I loved to treat with disdain, considering him too cold, pessimistic, and morbid. Now, I understood that the limitation was mine, not his. Clinging to the most ordinary problems, I'd scoffed at the Irishman and at her, my mother. Jackass. Maria Amélia had said she remembered that morning, she had left the house early, using a blouse she'd received as a birthday present from a former student. Later, she could only remember the moment at the beach, surrounded by strangers, and the solitude; a packed Hospital Miguel Couto, the hallway, me coming to get her. She had confused me with my father, I took the risk of telling her, and she answered *Are you serious?* She turned toward the window. *Do you think I was in the building?* she wondered, *in the hallway in my dream? Maybe you were*, I responded, promising to get her out of there and take her home. Maria Amélia accepted without argument, conscious that she could no longer trust herself. She got up to brush her teeth. I stayed sitting there, exhausted. I was such a shallow actor. I should have given my Lear the same depth that she possessed, but I was too vain to understand the exile of one's ego. As I waited for my mother to come out of the bathroom, I doubted whether I had ever arrived at the essence of my profession.

WHEN I WAS STILL an understudy, acting, to me, was a catharsis connected more to the gratification of my own senses than to those who took the time to listen to me. I ignored the audience. That's how it was in college, that's how it was at the Crato and at the Ipanema. This beginner's deafness erected the fourth wall, the stupid gusto of one with loads of hormones to ensure his chest is always puffed up and nothing more. My symptoms worsened during a period when I wandered aimlessly, after Rubens and Ivan went away. I even paid them a visit them in Friburgo, I was invited to join their rural community, but I was a young man, and I had my ambitions. I was part of an amateur group, I played the little king who couldn't get it up in the worst sort of children's theater productions, I was refused by the Teatro Asdrúbla, and faltered at TV auditions.

That's when a fury spread throughout Rio's theatrical class.

Ernesto Guria, the avant-garde Argentine film director, fleeing the hard-line government of our neighboring country, had made his way to Europe, where he'd forged important partnerships with the high priests of experimental theater. He'd participated as an understudy in the Peter Brook version of *A Midsummer Night's Dream*, had met Grotowski, and become friends with Julian Beck and Judith Malina in Paris, all this before the Living Theatre made its way to Brazil. It was the legendary couple that convinced him to come here, spurred by a partnership with the Teatro Oficina, workshops in the favelas of São Paulo and a prison in Minas, where they ended up after being caught with pot in a hotel in Ouro Preto.

The fact that José Celso Martinez Corrêa, the Oficina's shaman, kept his distance weighed on me like failure. The Ipanema was the closest I got to the aesthetic revolution that was taking place in the most violent way in the city of São Paulo. The gentle sway of the sea influenced Rio's theater scene to the same degree that São Paulo's formal roughness acted upon José Celso's hard-hitting style. Perhaps out of a desire to plant his flag on an uncharted beach, Guria had chosen to reign in Copacabana. The director hadn't cut ties with the so-called bourgeois theater; he performed in conventional spaces, never on the street, he hemmed closer to the text more than he relied on improvisation, and he had a sophisticated understanding of the system of lighting and sound devices. Prohibited from setting foot in his beloved Buenos Aires—the snake-eating hermanos somehow managed to be even worse than our own camo-toting gorillas—and making the most of the mystique of the exiled intellectual, the *porteño* landed in Guanabara Bay already deified.

Answering the open call for a workshop that would lead to the selection of actors for his first production, Jackson and I hurried to the Teatro Cacilda Becker in Catete to try our luck. My legs buckled when the mythic director's shadow appeared among the chairs. Short, wearing knee-high boots and a wine-colored turtleneck, Guria sported a long black wig, pulled back into a ponytail, a mix between Carlos Gardel and Sitting Bull. A ceremonious man, he took slow steps toward the middle of the stage, trailed by his French assistant, a skinny brunette who served as his page. He gave a quick wave and lit up a Minister while looking into the eyes of each of the nearly seventy actors present. We froze in anticipation. Guria snuffed out his cigarette in a portable ashtray and told everyone to take off their clothes.

We obeyed immediately, to make clear our wholehearted commitment. We were used to it. Getting naked was part of the preliminary test in any introductory course. A reaction to the terror imposed on the planet by the Cold War, which provoked drastic reactions in politics, arts, and social life. Things were so rough that a sensitive young man like me either had the bravura to join up with the armed resistance or embarked on an artistic career, no less radical, using his body as a form of protest. We rubbed our nether regions all over filthy theaters, the real pain was actual threats, we licked one another's sweat without betraying disgust, we kissed on the mouth, we simulated sex, or even consummated it, without ever holding back. Nudity was the first condition, sine qua non, to proving yourself as an actor.

After we'd freed ourselves of our clothing, Guria told us to wander, filling the empty spaces in the theater. The Olive Oyl of the French Quarter joined the group and had us all form a circle. We let go of one another's hands and lay down on the floor, as we were told, our feet just barely touching. *Inhale, exhale*, the Pope commanded in Spanish, and our work began. *What is essential today is to know what we are fighting against, to recognize the formal, social, and political structures that impede sensual freedom, empathic fluidity, and the peace that one longs for*, and then he hummed a long OM like an oriental monk. We did the same in chorus. The mantra reverberated throughout the walls of the theater and the old Teatro Cacilda Becker suddenly felt like a Buddhist temple. Once the sacred atmosphere had been established, the director asked us to focus our thoughts on something that we found threatening. *Now with the image formed*, he said, *scream at the oppressor with all the force of your lungs*. I concentrated as hard as I could and pictured, from the depths of my soul, our dictator Garrastazú Médici emerging covered in medals, dark glasses, and a military kepi. The specter was proof of my nonconformism. I was proud of myself. I was already preparing to exorcize the general when the scowling general suddenly became blurry, giving way to the tender profile of my deceased grandfather, a stand-up gentleman whom I truly admired. Without the time to find a substitute, and fearful of earning a big fat zero on this test, I threw all my voodoo at the old man. If someone asked, I would lie, say I'd excommunicated the dictator. *Stand*, the guide instructed us, *approach*. We closed the circle, forming a human lizard, my rear rubbing up against the belly of the short girl behind me, my dick in the back of the guy in front of me; no risk of an erection there, *Hair* had already taught me to control it. *OOOMMM* ... we returned to the tribal chant. The French girl directed us with her hands to sit in a circle while Guria explained the next

95

exercise. We ought to, one by one, assume position in the center of the circle, screaming the first word that came to mind until we'd formed a gear. My prima donna instincts overtook me. He'd barely finished his explanation when I jumped, all six feet of me, to the middle of the circle and with hand raised to the sky, I blurted *GOD!* inspired by my comrades' *OOOMMM.* The tableau was set. Little by little, everyone assumed their places, some in prayer position, screaming *FEAR! TRUTH! SUBMISSION!* Others in a full-on attack upon the deity, bellowing *DEATH! LIES! HALLUCINATION!* I could have sworn that I'd attracted the attention of the *gran señor*. It ended with me surrounded by the circle of participants. Guria gave the order *al piso!* and we fell to the floor. The slimy mass of loins, asses, and armpits collapsed over the stage, opening the way to the heavy petting. We were also used to this. Any high-school theater knew the routine of the hedonist amoeba. I looked for Jackson as soon as I realized where things were going. We had suffered our share of unwanted advances. The solution was to agree that, every time we got a whiff of coming orgy, we'd find a way to band together, protecting ourselves from the barbarian horde. As soon as I found Jackson's heel, I scaled his thigh and we formed a shell, without revealing anxiety. Caught up in the sea of flesh, we writhed on the floor, feigning ecstasy. As we performed this affectionate ritual, Guria, his diction flawless, turned our attention to Chekhov.

"Millions of trees have perished. The homes of the wild animals and birds have been desolated; the rivers are shrinking, and many beautiful landscapes are gone forever. . . ."

His calming voice brought peace to the hive, the frenzy soon abated, and his assistant set to untangling the human knot. I was sprawled on the floor, my eyes closed. I knew *The Seagull* by heart, we all wanted to be Treplev, the hero who attempts suicide, but I'd skipped over *Uncle Vanya*, *The Cherry Orchard*, and *Three Sisters*.

Guria had a keen understanding of the scene. He put on some Chopin and left us there, prostrate. This intermission lasted an eternity, I fell asleep, I have no idea for how long. The squalid French girl's sexy voice whispered in my ear telling me to stand up and get dressed. While I steadied myself to put on my underwear, I noted that my competition had been reduced to thirteen other young men and seven girls, the others had been sent away. Jackson among them. I felt for my partner, admiring the elegant manner in which Guria had conducted the cuts. Those who remained fought their way to a brief interview. I was last. I sat before him there in row D of the Cacilda, I was tense and sweaty, my lips trembled. Guria flashed an enigmatic smile, his eyes locked on mine. Later, I understood it was his way of asserting control over the conversation. He took his time sharing his ideas to create suspense, which kept his inter-locutor at his mercy. I smiled back, lowered my head, and an immediate empathy settled between us. It was like a courtship, and we were in love, I think. Guria revealed his plans to stage *Uncle Vanya* in Brazil, mentioned the Amazon and our natural riches, and asked if I knew the play. I thought about lying, but I decided to be honest, my blank expression telegraphing my negative response. My honesty earned me one more look of approval, the test was going well. *Russia is very close to Brazil*, he said, *the vast territory, the late end of slavery*. I didn't speak, only listened, worried about appearing naive, about disappointing him, about being who I was. Guria uttered unexpected praise, confiding that I'd impressed him. I blushed. He handed me a photocopy containing the same text we'd just heard from his lips, asking me to read it out loud.

"*THE RUSSIAN FORESTS*," I began, bellowing.

"Shhhh," he interrupted. "Speak for yourself and for me."

Guria asked for tenderness, something no one had ever demanded of me. For the preceding five years, I had dedicated myself to cursing the injustice of the world, spewing righteous indignation, bursting with textbook joy. I was an extra at the Ipanema, I had never faced a true director, and was discovering, there during the test with the Argentine that I had completely overlooked what my job was. I would have given my life for the Shaman of the Pampas' blessing. Being chosen by Guria meant the opportunity to be rescued from the chorus of true believers, the whole host of the angry, the freethinkers, the folklore activism would be within reach. Fear, surprise, joy, hate, disgust, and sadness, that was my range as an actor, the basic emotions any child can imitate; but infinite sentiments exist between these, beyond these, the finer points of my profession, I was entering unfamiliar territory.

"The Russian forests," I repeated softly, and he yelled *Bravo!* I drank it all in. *I heard the words in silence, before being free of them*, he explained, *pause, create an image, look and only then continue onward. Let me see, come to me*. It was a more elevated form of the primal scream I had just released against my dear old grandfather. *The abodes of the animals, the birds, the rivers, are not unknown to one who was born here*, he said. *It would be so much simpler to take off all my clothes and curse*, I thought, taking a few more cautious steps. Slowly, the text's meaning opened like a flower. With each subject, verb, and predicate conquered, I sought reassurance in Guria's expression and he nodded affirmatively. For the first time, I found myself before an auteur. Eureka. *Shouting is easy, Mario, what is difficult it is to be born into hearing; and you will not be, if you do not understand what you say*, he concluded. I felt like begging for the role. The feeling of taking an important step in that trade, of kissing grade school goodbye, of never again having to graze with the herd.

Work begins in two months. My invitation was sealed.

Leaving the Cacilda, out among the passersby in Catete, I looked at the text to count how many lines I would have. Ignorant, I didn't know the dimensions of Astrov, alter ego to Chekhov, a doctor, like the author, a nature lover, a passionate drunk, central character in *Vanya*. Guria had seen a leading man in me. I sat on the sidewalk and hiccupped with joy.

†

What came next was one those rare miracles, complete happiness, free of all frustration. A state of grace that would never repeat itself at the same voltage, and of which I still harbor a nostalgia that knows no limits. My Astrov took the Tupi theater scene by storm. Five months after that first meeting, I was transformed into a god beneath the spotlight, a counterculture sex symbol, archetype of the ideal man, Dionysus reborn. Guria ran a considerable risk in tapping me. I was an immature actor surrounded by an experienced cast who didn't have time to waste with me. Of the seventy candidates who auditioned, four had survived, me and three others who were assigned roles without any particular importance. I didn't have the age, the weight, or much less the understanding of my character's drunken nihilism. Guria demanded that I gain weight and let my beard grow, he saw Astrov as some enormous hibernating bear. In the mornings, I rehearsed naked in the Tijuca Forest, simulating an animal existence, and later I visited public hospitals, studying the doctors and their weariness. I began to drink, believing that the alcohol would only enhance my character. I delivered myself to Guria with a novice's blind devotion. After each rehearsal, he locked himself in a room with me and wore me out all night long. His demands bordered on cruelty. He grew irritated when I didn't deliver, he humiliated me in front of the other actors, alleging regrets, but, every now and then, he repaid me with a crumb of praise.

Lionized by the director, Ivo Nogueira, our Vanya, was a gem of an actor with a long history of supporting roles whom Guria had given a chance to take the lead. One awful day, when my porteño taskmaster threatened to replace me, Ivo pulled me out of the gutter. Distraught at not being up to the level of *El Genio*'s hallowed stagecraft, I grabbed my colleague in a tearful embrace, in the gutter just outside the actors' entrance. *Mario*, he said, *the man loves you, if he didn't love you, he wouldn't do what he does to you*. I was ready to throw in the towel. *The theater,* he said, *is a curious anomaly. Guria wants you to crawl, he's one of these directors that believes that an actor must suffer to leave behind the person he is,* Ivo explained. *It works. I don't know about with me, but I've seen it work. Guria has personally staked a lot on you as Astrov, hang in there,* he said, *hang in there because the laurels will come later. And if the opinion of a tired old actor is worth anything, you'll miss this torture one day.* Ivo was right, today all that's left is the memory of those *grands jetés,* the pirouettes, and giddiness of being onstage. And the love of the divine Helena played by Raquel Jablonovski, a stupendous actor, a stupendous lover. Whoever laid eyes on her never forgot her. I never did. My hopeless passion, my little she-devil, my ruination. And I, too, was her ruination.

Raquel made for a devious, evasive, seductive Helena. In the beginning, we barely looked at each other. We read the text from across the table, our faces turned to the script. My impression was that she had no respect for me. Intimidated, I felt cornered before the sphinx. With enough charisma to be convincing during the long monologues during which Astrov reflects on poverty in the countryside and the destruction of nature, I was incapable of wooing her, let alone achieving the doctor's ironic yearning for his beloved. When the time came to get the show on the road, I had to face her. After a few frustrated attempts, Raquel suggested we jump to the scene where Astrov declares his love for Helena, just the two of us, without Guria. I arrived early. She was waiting. Raquel walked up to me with a gift. Ice in her voice, she told me to open it. It was a collared shirt, a linen suit, and leather shoes. *Astrov is a man*, she said, *dressing the way you do isn't going to help you*. I glanced at my torn jeans, my old tennis shoes, the teenage T-shirt, and I was ashamed. She was right. I smiled timidly and made to leave, but she asked me to change right there in front of her. *Be a man*, she said. I went silent, the atmosphere was heavy. *Be my man*, she said. My cock grew hard, it was out of my control. Slowly, I removed my shirt. We stood there, muted by libido. I completed the ritual, taking off my tennis shoes, socks, and finally, my pants. My firm body in full view. Her eyes scanned my chest, my cock. *Just a couple more questions, and that's the end*, she said, using a phrase from the text. *Let's speak frankly . . .* she continued. *It's about my stepdaughter, do you like her? No*, I responded frankly, I felt no attraction for the Sonya played by Bia Alencar, the ugly and profound Bia, whom the market had tossed aside for her lack of sex appeal. I didn't feel a thing for her, my goosebumps were testament to that. Raquel handed me my pants. I got dressed. *One more word . . .* she said, moving through her lines. Less vulnerable, I faced her as an equal. Raquel was as attracted to me as I was to her, I had discovered that day. This abolished our difference in age, talent, fame. We were two identical animals. *My sweet tigress, don't look at me that way*, I rejoindered, *I am an old bird*. And Raquel handed me my bunched-up dress shirt, satisfied with her Astrov. *You know perfectly well what brings me here, beautiful, sleek tigress*, I continued. *For a whole month I have done nothing but seek you eagerly . . .* and I stepped in for a kiss, without knowing anymore what was real and what was theater. The world was spinning, the theater. We were interrupted by

Guria at the height of our game—otherwise, it all would have become very real. We killed it during that afternoon's rehearsal, alarmed at the intensity of our feelings. We never spoke about what happened that day. There was no need. Feeding on our furious attraction, we preferred to keep it for the stage. And we did well to do so. We waited the whole afternoon for that evening's encounter, we kept a respectful distance backstage so as to devour each other onstage, in front of the others, aroused by the exhibitionism the theater allowed. Guria taught me a great deal, but Raquel taught me everything. How to be a man, how to test the boundaries that separate the actor from his role.

The set was made up of a forest of soft, white trunks with an enormous mirror at the back, which multiplied the rows of trees. Not a trace of leaves or branches, everything barren, the bare essentials. The columns also served to imitate the inside of the house, not a single wall, door, curtain, no excess. I wore a wrinkled suit that recalled the one Raquel had given me, and I used it during the entire rehearsal. I wore a leather satchel across my shoulder. The physical demands doubled the size of my chest, the primal screams during the jungle workshops had intensified my already low voice. I became the sweet and violent bear that Guria had always imagined me to be. Raquel paraded in a long linen dress and a silk shirt buttoned up to the neck, with a thick lace that came undone with each act. Vanya, threadbare pajamas. A refined minimalism. Guria would have spit upon the hairy sheep of Stein's color guard.

My Lear was a result of that Astrov, of the desire to relive it. I wasn't old enough for the role, not Astrov, not Lear, but

I believed I could be blessed twice. I was not. It's chance that makes the final call. Never again. I could feel the audience teeming with excitement each time I appeared, their atomic silences. I anticipated each cough, I mastered the timing of each laugh, each sigh, my voice embracing the entire theater, filling it, as though it were something I could grab hold of. My god, how I miss those days. Before the curtain opened, locked in the silence of my dressing room, I looked myself in the mirror, barely believing my luck, bursting with joy, savage, in love. Astrov, Astrov, Astrov, something much greater than me, a supreme being whose stature I had managed to reach. The applause counted for something, no doubt, but it's those moments in the dressing room that I most remember, the smell backstage, the warm breath of my Helena and the copy of the script I stuffed in my leather satchel, to remind myself how it all began. All of Rio wanted to sleep with me. In a single week, there was a line around the block, women, girls, boys, everyone outside wanted us. The hushed murmurs at Fiorentina each time we entered the dining room for endless meals after the show. The recognition of our colleagues. But none of this compares to the excitement onstage, the sensation of being free of myself, of being somebody else, of being whomever I wanted, whatever I wanted, when I wanted. I thought it would always be like that, but no. *The first years are easy, the hard part is persevering*, says Nina, the heroine of *The Seagull*. Chekhov knew, it's difficult to reinvent yourself at sixty. I couldn't do it.

†

Guria was waiting for me backstage after the premiere. He was smiling proudly at his Galatea. I walked over to him, gave him a hug, and was overcome by a flood of tears as I clutched the despot. I kissed him on the mouth, told him I owed him an eternal debt. Guria patted my head, he treated me like scum but also like a son. *Everything will be very fast*, he said, *don't lose yourself, take care.* Then he became serious and added, *Only in theater you will be free, Mario, in this horror called theater, do not forget.* And he told me that his bags were packed, he would be leaving Brazil. He'd received an invitation to take up a residency in Italy, at a center for theater research in the countryside. He'd thought about inviting me along, but the language barrier would mean going back twenty spaces and he didn't want that for me. My heart froze, I stared at him in panic, I was losing a father, this demonic father. *The world begins to open up for you, Mario, cultivate the talent that you have, and never confuse movement and action.*

For a long time, I was faithful to my taskmaster's advice. We traveled all over Brazil with *Vanya*. For the first time, I set foot in the finest theaters. I learned to adjust my body and voice to the immensity of their spaces. When I returned to Rio, to close out the adventure with a sold-out run at the Teatro João Caetano, I was already a celebrated actor. More invitations followed. I left the closet I'd been splitting with Jackson and the musician couple and moved to a one-bedroom in Ipanema. Fulfilling the promise I'd made to Guria, I was living off my work, I could barely believe it.

†

During the final performance, we held hands and waited for the curtain to close, after an intoxicating ovation. We formed a circle and embraced, inconsolable. Nevermore. We welcomed friends onstage, we proposed a toast to the end of the show, and we all returned to our dressing rooms. I stayed behind. Beneath the ugly service light, the stagehands began breaking down the set. The tree trunks fell with a thud, one after the other. Scorched earth. *Each day there are fewer and fewer forests*—Guria's voice echoed in my memory. I was now an orphan of my own forest. I went to change, Ivo had already left, we scheduled the final banquet at Fiorentina. Searching before the mirror, I didn't know what to do with myself without my Astrov. I gathered my belongings scattered across the table, the used makeup, the cards, the flowers, the photos. I stopped. I felt hopeless. I fell apart. The door opened. It was her. Raquel. The sound of her breath, the perfume, I didn't need to turn around to know it was her. We didn't say a word, I knew why she was there, and I thanked God she was, because the idea of not seeing her onstage at night frightened me as much, or more, than going back to being myself. Raquel walked up to me, slowly, placed her hands on my shoulders, her slender fingers, her thin wrists. I held them between mine and we remained frozen there for minutes, in silence, aware that we owed each other an intimate adieu. I jumped up, grabbed her by the waist, and we sank into a frantic kiss. There was no more Astrov or Helena, it was me and her mourning their loss. We rolled around the dusty dressing room beneath the weight of a year of anticipation. For the first time we touched each other without them. Actually, Chekhov was present, as he always was, multiplying our fantasy by a thousand. The Russians boning like mad. When it was over, we laid there in each other's arms, eyes closed, knowing that what awaited us outside could never compete with what had transpired between us.

"*A Razor in the Flesh*," Raquel whispered, as though proposing we run away. "Rehearsals begin in a month, I suggested you, they already accepted."

MY MOTHER came out of the bathroom ready for bed. It took me a few minutes to snap out of my trance, I was surprised at having unearthed the ghost of Raquel. I'd managed for decades not to deal with that disastrous love affair. They both filled me with dread, Maria Amélia and Raquel, and one now had elicited the other. My mother sat down on the bed, she was no longer the same person I'd been speaking with a short time earlier. It was the wife that looked at me now. She looked sad. I got up to help her and felt her hand squeeze my arm. She pulled me to her and whispered that, one day, life would bring us a child. *It just wasn't the right time*, she said, downcast, and rested her head against my chest. She thought she'd been hospitalized after losing a child. Maternal insanity. It was as though something inside me broke each time Maria Amélia floated off. *Death would be less cruel*, I thought, guilty for wishing for her end. Stepping into my role as husband, I hugged her warily, assuring her that, one day, there was no doubt, we would have a child. I waited for her to relax and called the doctor, demanded that they sedate her. The nurse administered the dose and took care of the wound around my eye. I thanked her. I passed the time until the sun came up planning next steps. Over time, I would empty the large apartment where Maria Amélia had lived, selling what didn't fit at home, and would rent it out to help with my expenses.

The next morning, we left the hospital and set out for our new life.

On the way, she asked to pass by the Jardim Botânico. She wanted to look at the school and house that had appeared in her dream. Two buildings of frosted glass occupied not only the place of the school but that of the old German-style house. My mother didn't say a word, she merely moved in close to me, growing sadder and sadder, and ordered the driver on. It hadn't been a dream, I now understood. Before drowning herself, the most likely scenario is that she had wandered alone through the places she had lived and, only later, thrown herself into the sea. Perhaps she didn't know it, but an important part of her longed to die. To put an end to her life. As Raquel had done. I couldn't let that happen. Not again.

†

Maria Amélia grew quiet when I opened her front door. When still sane, she visited me rarely, it was normal for me to go see her at her apartment in Copacabana. She asked why I had plastered over the wall of exposed brick. I suspected that she and my father had lived in such an environment, before I had ever existed. I made up some story about a renovation. *I want to begin from scratch*, I said, *the loss wasn't easy for me*. I pretended my low spirits were on account of the miscarriage that never was. She understood. I noticed that Maria Amélia grew calmer at seeing me vulnerable, perhaps it was the last relic of motherhood that still survived within her. I began to use this often. Any time we began to approach an argument, I backed off, wounded, and she likewise showed restraint. It was a great antidote. She wanted to know about the maid, I avoided reminding her of the woman's heart attack and pretended she was still on vacation in the North, visiting her family. Maria Amélia bought into my lie. I'd begun to master the role.

I set up my mother in front of the television and locked myself in the bedroom. I called Gomes. He asked for time to close out the remaining accounts for the Ministry and advised me to look for a job. *We've got a shortfall*, he said, *it's best to prepare yourself*. I needed to find someone to take care of Maria Amélia, wait for the swelling around my eye to diminish, and find a job. I swore to take it in stages. I gave my mother a sleeping pill, tucked her in the middle bedroom down the hallway, waited for her to doze off, and then went to bed. I thought of Raquel. I missed her, I missed me, and the tempest at the end.

FUNERAL REFRESHMENTS for Astrov and Helena were served cold at the first rehearsal of Vado and Neusa Sueli. The change seemed promising. We had abandoned the melancholy of the Russian steppes for the hysteria of national poverty. I refused tempting offers, films, contracts. I didn't care about the pitiful director, the poor production values, and the tinderbox theater, we would be together, in the ring, arms locked in the chaos of Plínio Marcos's making.

The play is about twenty-four hellish hours in the life of a prostitute and her pimp in the Baixo Paulista. The opposite of what we had been up until then. My sleazeball character flourished without much effort. I played nice, nasty, sarcastic, in the same line as Jece Valadão, whom I had seen in the scum's skin in an old film from 1969. Jece didn't play a character, he was the character. And so would I be, no screaming, no exaggeration. Vado cured me of Astrov. Adieu prophetic hero, bring on the damn creep. I was pleased with my choice. Neusa Sueli, on the other hand, made my partner sick to her stomach. Raquel was just masochistic enough to take on the collapse of Plínio's whore, that's why she'd agreed to the role, but in practice, she felt disgust for her character's degeneracy. After a month of readings, when we began to take the production to the stage, her aversion became explicit. Filled with regret and lacking the courage to ask someone else to take over, she took to humiliating the director, the team, she was like a caged cat. The fleeting nobility of her Helena in *Vanya* vanished completely and suddenly there emerged from within that delicate woman a hateful creature that chose me for its punching bag. Raquel mocked me, calling me a boutique gigolo, she plotted to pull me off my pedestal. She pretended there was nothing wrong between us. I wanted to throw her from the stage each time she interrupted the proceedings, calling me an amateur, a boy, demanding we start from the beginning. *Da capo!* she'd whine. She was begging to be hit. I hit her, kicked her, dragged her by the hair in my fury, but it wasn't enough, nothing was enough. Without a trace of our former idyll, we were headed for a colossal comedown. During the sixth week of this endurance test, she squeezed into a taxi with me after a rehearsal in which she regaled me with derision and took her nails to my arm and neck. She wore an erotic smile and told the driver to head for Lapa. *I'm tired of lying*, she said. She was crazy, Raquel, a suicidal actress, the kind who goes nuts on account of a role. We got off in front of a bar, she greeted the streetwalkers. I discovered she'd been doing a bit of *trottoir* there since rehearsals had begun. We climbed the dark stairway and sat in a corner. We drank and smoked, observing the Vados and Neusas Suelis of the musty lupanar. *Can you get syphilis by osmosis?* I asked. On her fifth glass of Paraguayan whiskey, she stuck her hand down my fly and the night ended with an insane fuck on the sofa in her apartment. The sun already up, Raquel turned on her side and slept. It had been a long time since I'd seen her sated like that. We woke up in the late afternoon, late to work. I ran to the shower, but she stood in my way, saying that Neusa Sueli liked the smell of me. I didn't argue, I'd become a slave to her desires. Our exhaustion turned up the heat; partners in crime, we were nearing the scene where Vado and Neusa Sueli accuse their queer neighbor of stealing the money they keep in their nightstand. We descended on the poor guy like birds of prey. When the day was over, I thought I deserved some rest, but Raquel wanted another go-round. So off we went to the red-light district, on a mission to pull another spurious all-nighter, followed by sex that reeked of cachaça. And that's how things went, *ad eternum*. We'd go till morning, befouled from our orgy, and wake up after sunset, just before it was time to lay it all out on the cramped stage. A week before the premiere, the game had turned in her favor. Raquel had won, she dominated the scene, held the reins of fate. Completely spent, I was thrown off my game, at the mercy of her whims. My Vado morphed into a eunuch. Our companionship soon gave way to virulent competition. We attacked each other for nothing, a couple at the end of the line, and I was getting the shorter end. One night, I left the theater distraught, Raquel had thrown a fit because I'd squeezed her chin too hard during a scene in which I call her an old hag. The problem wasn't her chin, I knew, it was the old hag. I'd discovered her secret weakness. Like Neusa Sueli, Raquel had reached the age of forty and begun to lose roles to younger women, she was ready to go for plastic surgery, she was terrified of growing old. My twenty-seven years were an insult to her. No matter how much she nursed her neurosis, she knew that it was this sucker who would make it out of that play in one piece. Vado abandons the harlot in bed, after the false promise of a fuck, and then walks out the door with a swagger, ready for the next in line. Neusa Sueli can only go to the threshold and ask helplessly: *Are you coming back?* Raquel couldn't stand that. I waited for her to quit whining about how I'd dislocated her jaw, grabbed my things, and walked out without looking back. The specter showed up in a taxi. *One last time before the premiere*, she said, all meek. She was scared, she'd noticed the change in me. We walked to the front of the old two-story house in the city center, it was a hot March night, the street reeked of trash. We sat at a table in the back without saying a word. She hit the bottle hard, danced with whores, looking straight at me, until we lost sight of one another. I thought Raquel had left, jilting me as revenge. I considered taking off, but my exhaustion proved stronger. I stayed where I was, sulking, watching a trollop past her prime perform an awkward striptease; I moaned to the sound of Odair José's bordello bolero coming from the record player, *I'm gonna take you far from here* . . . and I perked up at the idea of using the song at the end of the performance. That's when Raquel came my way from the end of the bar, dragging some freak on her arm. *He wants to know how much*, she said. I didn't catch it. *This gentleman here wants to know how much and I explained that you're the one to talk to*, she continued. I laughed, thinking the joke would end there. *We're already done for today*, I responded, grabbing her hand, burning to get out of that place. Raquel didn't budge. *He doesn't mind if you watch*, she said in a direct challenge. I froze. If I backed down, my Vado would be buried once and for all. *Thirty*, I ventured, *twenty minutes, thirty bucks*. The man grabbed a few bills from his pocket and handed them to me. *Checkmate*, I thought, *she won't go through with it*. But the madwoman grabbed the freak by the arm, took the lead, and headed for the stairs. I went after them, holding the handrail, woozy from the trail of cheap deodorant wafting from the greaser. He was a kid, solidly built, his hair standing on end with hair gel and sweat stains beneath his armpits. Raquel walked into the first cheap hotel she could find, paid for an hour up front, and took the elevator. I thought about taking a walk around the block, leaving her alone with her lab rat and her method acting bullshit, but what would my Vado be the next day? We walked into the room. I closed the door and stood there in disbelief. Raquel, on her knees, took Shorty's belt off and sucked his dick in a trancelike state of pure devotion. A strange sort of arousal rose up until it reached my ear, I felt jealous, disgusted. The billy goat released a sickening grunt as he came and I considered our little orgy over. I shoved the dog outside, slid the lock on the door, and faced the lioness. Raquel, still on her knees, laughed in my face. *Hi*, she said, *you're still here? What do you think?* I answered. *You never get home this early. That's because I'm not getting home, you cow, I haven't even left yet*, I snapped back, moving through the script, I already knew this routine. *Are you sick? Sick, my ass. Calm down, there's no need to get upset* . . . she continued, buttoning up her blouse with a sly

115

expression. *You think you're funny? I'm going to fill your face with all sorts of joy.* I twisted her arm, I was merciless. *You're hurting me. You haven't seen nothing yet, you slut.* I yanked Raquel up from the floor and threw her bodily onto the coil-spring mattress. I mounted her from behind, clamping down on her hands with my legs, Raquel writhing like a defiled virgin. Neusa Sueli. I slapped her across the face, trying to exorcize the demon. *Where's the money*, I said, *where's the money?* The lines coming one after the other, we were ready for the curtain to open. In the final scene, Neusa Sueli complains that Vado no longer comes around. He promises a scrap of their former love but then bolts without consummating the act. And that's exactly what I did, I left Raquel sprawled on the bed in that hellhole. When I made it to the brink of that pestilent loft, before a rusty sign with the warning that it was illegal to mess around in the hallway, I heard the last breath of the play: *Are you coming back?*

No, Raquel, I'm not coming back.

†

Opening night came four days later. The final run-up made the director's jaw drop. She was right, I'll give her that. Without it all, my Vado would have been nothing more than a small-time sponger. Now, I would lock myself in the dressing room without looking at her face, once again saving everything for the stage. Yan Michalski sung our praises, dedicating the entire first page of the entertainment section to our debacle. The tight little theater obliged the spectators to protect themselves from the spitting, the punching, and the kicking. Some got up and left, indignant, demanding a refund. It was a scandal. If Astrov had appealed to the libido of the most sensitive, Vado had them lining up around the block. That was my revenge. Every day I left with one, two, three women. She started to drink, do drugs, she withered. Neusa Sueli was the end of her.

The theater is a perilous profession, you either keep your characters at arm's length or you burn yourself alive, which is what Raquel did. I also suffered the aftereffects of Plínio's pimp. I became a vile motherfucker, I no longer believed in love, a real dreg of humanity. A consistent tan, foreign cologne, and shirt unbuttoned to display my chest hair. The triumph of youth. The pleasure of hearing her call for me, as the lights went out. *Are you coming back?*

No, Raquel, I'm not.

She tried to act like she didn't care. She accepted the courtship of a rainmaker from São Paulo's vice district. The gangster promised her the moon and more for one of those eroto-intellectual films they were making at the time. He wanted the two us together on tape, but she preferred someone else, I didn't sweat it. We met our obligations for six months in Rio and another six in São Paulo. Sworn enemies onstage and off. We ended up cutting all ties, tired of so much theater. She got a new start as the star of the upscale end of the Pornochanchada industry and I headed for the coast of Bahia. I'd decided to take a vacation, before shutting myself away on a farm in a remote area of that state to live as Riobaldo in a Cinema Novo version of João Guimarães Rosa's *Devil to Pay in the Backlands* that only ever existed on paper.

I went to see her onscreen when I came back from Bahia.

Adelle was an atrocious film, a mash-up of Bergman with *Emmanuelle*. Raquel walks around naked for most of the film, in the role of a socialite who, after years fulfilling the fetishes of the bourgeoisie, is co-opted by the guerrilla movement and finds love with a woman activist from São Paulo's industrial belt. In a hideous scene, the two of them screw in the open, the camera hanging from the ceiling. After endless moaning, the couple pretend to reach orgasm in unison, Raquel twisting from side to side, a histrionic beyond hope, before lighting a cigarette and walking to the window, reciting some incomprehensible paragraph from Schopenhauer, or something to that effect. Prayer time at an end, Raquel whispers in her girlfriend's ear, *Love, come to bed, I'm horny as hell*, and the two of them go back to their pathetic bunga-bunga. The only reason I didn't get up and leave was because the sequence is followed by some cops from the secret police machine-gunning the hideout of an alleged communist cell, riddling her leftist girlfriend with bullets. Raquel feigns tears over the martyr's bloodied body, and then, without any plausible explanation, runs naked along a deserted beach, writhing in the sand like a beef à Milanesa wracked with depression. I felt nauseous as I left the theater, trying to comprehend why she would have submitted herself to vulgarity masquerading as political resistance. The actresses had subjected themselves to all sorts of exploitation, convinced that taking their clothes off was a liberating act. The launch included the cover of the largest men's magazine at the time. I leafed through the pages, with gynecological photos of Raquel from every angle, her face faking a cheap orgasm. I wanted to ask her why but didn't have the courage.

I returned home with the wrinkled magazine in my hands. I tried to calm down but couldn't. When night had fallen, I grabbed a taxi and knocked on her door without calling. I furiously rang the doorbell, a startled Raquel answered, she was skinny, used up. *Is this what you want to do with yourself?* I attacked, wanting to rub her nose in the magazine. Raquel pushed me back toward the door, screaming at me to go away. I forced my way in, hurling insults over that vulgar film, mocked her run along the beach, I imitated her fuck with her fifth-rate co-star, asked her how much they had paid her for the porno shoot. Raquel growled through her teeth, telling me I had no right to stick my nose in her business, that she was much happier than she was with me at that tinderbox theater. She demanded I get out. I called her a slut and she called me an animal. Suddenly, we both went quiet. Raquel started to cry, so did I, I shed tears of horror, kneeling at her feet. I asked why. *Leave me alone, Mario,* she begged, *leave me alone, there's no fixing me, get out of here, I don't know what to do with myself.* Raquel's body sagged, her shoulders slumping, her face hidden behind a wall of hair. I embraced her, told her I loved her, asked her what was going on. *Nothing,* she said, *it's me. I have no talent for life. What do you mean?* I asked. And I kissed her all over, as though it could cure her. We screwed. We screwed sweetly, as we'd rarely done up until that point. With tenderness. We slept side by side, at peace. When I woke up, she brought me coffee. She promised to take care of herself, to call me when she was feeling better. I persisted, asking her what was wrong. She didn't want to tell me, she didn't ask for help as she should have.

Six months later, Raquel would once again make the headlines. Dead. Her tumultuous relationship with the Almighty of the Baixo Paulista, the despicable producer who had convinced her to become the sex symbol of the vice district's intellectual wing, had ended in tragedy. Raquel had betrayed him with the heartthrob from *Adelle*, a vile character, a nasty individual known for his high tolerance for all types of drugs. Offended, the Godfather delivered photographs of her partying hard with the porno star to the tabloids. That's what she hadn't wanted to tell me the night I tried to help, she had been blackmailed. She was ashamed. Raquel locked herself away at VIPs, a motel along Avenida Niemeyer, and went three sleepless nights with the doped-up asshole. On the last night, he walked out the door and she jumped out the window. She couldn't handle another Vado. In the retrospectives published in the newspapers, there we were, she and I, Astrov and Helena, Vado and Neusa Sueli. I felt a terrible sense of guilt, as though I'd been responsible for that woman's fall from grace.

Raquel's suicide is what made me leave the theater. The curse of being onstage. I swore I'd never love an actress again. To be honest, I never loved anyone again, not the same way, not with that fury, not to that degree.

CARINE, MY UNEMPLOYED COUSIN, agreed to hold down the fort in my absence. We set a reasonable salary, without benefits. The day she saw her planted in the living room, Maria Amélia nearly went crazy with jealousy. It was no use mentioning my aunt, my grandmother, my cousins. Possessed, she slammed the bedroom door and paced around the room. I slipped back into my role, I raised my voice, playing the wounded husband, and screamed that I wasn't the kind of man to have an affair with my own niece. She suddenly stopped her pacing, her face, her mouth, her eyes popping out of her head; it suddenly clicked, or nearly anyway. *Is that Carine?* she asked, perplexed. *Yes!* I answered back, *it's Carine, the daughter of your sister-in-law Neusa. She's so grown up . . .* she said and turned around to greet her visitor.

I oriented my cousin in her daily toils, I asked her to never contradict Maria Amélia, or laugh at my role as husband. Carine didn't care if she was in Tijuca or there, since she spent hours on end in front of the TV. She hadn't succumbed to the lure of social media because her tight budget didn't allow for the luxury of a smartphone. She was overcome with agony at the least silence, and drove away her boredom by conversing out loud with whomever showed up on screen. Though she didn't cook, she wrote down recipes for lasagna, pavê, and pork ribs, fried on live television by the perky lady who hosted the morning programming; she followed the dog-eat-dog worlds of the afternoon variety shows and primped for the gala presentations, which stretched from six in the evening to eleven at night. I needed Carine more than she needed me, which is why I controlled my impulse to kick the shit out of that box, which was turned on twenty-four hours a day, even while she slept. My mother joined her in this habit. Finding both of them there at two in the morning, passed out in front of the TV, became commonplace. The new job gave structure to Carine's aimless existence, gave her a bit of money, and freed her from the family slum at Sáenz Peña, but the little princess never thanked me. Quite the opposite, she took over the apartment as though it were hers, hanging her panties on the shower faucet, leaving her flip-flops scattered around the living room, and to make sure her work wasn't confused with that of the cleaning lady, made it clear she wouldn't wash a single glass. I agreed. Carine could flood the bathroom, leave the frying pans filthy, swipe whatever she liked, as long as she met my mother's needs. Suspecting little missy of Tijuca of hereditary laziness, and worried she might drug Maria Amélia to ease the workload, I locked up all the medicines in a safe. They played cards, did crosswords together, read their horoscopes, became friends. Carine retouched Maria Amélia's hair coloring, while the elder gave her advice about marriage and children, though my cousin had neither.

The swelling had gone down around my eye, it was time to try to renew ties with the old TV station. Free of bruises and with my mother being watched, I followed Gomes's advice and tried to get my life back on track. I sought out a director, one of the old guard, whom I'd worked with during the golden years. *Mario*, he said, *you broke your contract, left singing a victory march, gave interviews calling everyone an idiot, they put you on ice, my friend, they'll forget before long, but for now*, he advised, *it's better to dock in another port*. In the last year, a third of the station's employees had been shown the door, he suspected there was a price on his head, and only didn't throw a fit because his long years of service guaranteed him a nice fat severance package that would take care of him until he was a very old man. *Theater* . . . he said, *what made you fall for such a thing?* Then he laughed, exclaiming *Oh, what a bore!* I pretended to agree and proudly said goodbye.

I went back through the turnstile hoping not to be seen, and I moaned, humiliated, cooking in the heat of a car beneath the midday sun. I just drove. I smoked nearly a pack of gold filters, my hands cycling between lighter, cigarette, and the wheel. I spoke to myself, cursed the world, I screamed until I'd convinced myself of the worst. Parked at the beach, I looked at the horizon, the beautiful afternoon coming to an end in the Barra da Tijuca, I threw the butt on the floor and appealed to divine intervention. I grabbed the telephone and began to dial. Lineu answered. Health restored, my stage mate, eyewitness to my disastrous *Lear*, was preparing for the shooting of the biblical drama at a competing network. He was happy, I'd even

123

say radiant. It caught me off guard, I'd never seen him like that. Was it some miracle? Perhaps. After the sudden death of a colleague of the same generation, he was elevated to the role of Abraham, patriarch of the chosen people. He made a point to go to the funeral to thank the dead man. *It was God who commissioned the heart attack*, he said.

The idea behind *Sodom* was to knock the powerful network that had turned its back on me from its perch. Vengefully, I wanted to be part of this offensive. The writer promised to innovate, tempering religion, history, and science. Recent discoveries associated the collision of a supposed meteor with the Divine Fire of the Old Testament. They invested heavily in the theory, importing a Mexican from Hollywood to handle the special effects for the impact of the space rock in the soap opera's final phase. Lineu was overjoyed. *This pays much better than Shakespeare!* he gloated. *Were it not for your laugh-attack, Mario, I'd still be traipsing around in that diaper*, and we laughed unrestrained at the untimely incident. I didn't waste any time, there was no need to lie, Lineu was well aware of all my dirty laundry. *Any chance they need a pillar of salt?* I inquired. *Jesus loves you, my son, hurry up, they're already making invites*, he replied. This news revived my strength. I had led heavyweight casts on the top TV network and was still worth my weight in gold in the hands of the competition. It took a quick phone call to land a place of honor at the Last Supper. They fired the second-class actor who'd been brought on and offered me the role of Lot, nephew to the noble Abraham. I didn't feel bad about taking anyone's place, on the contrary, it was a sign of my street cred. After signing the contract, I sent an armful of roses to Lineu, together with a package of diapers. He got the joke.

Betraying Genesis, the soap version gave Lot a sinner's profile. Joined by his ambitious wife and two attractive daughters, he abandons his saintly uncle someplace between Haram and the Promised Land, to settle down in the most corrupt stretch of the Fertile Crescent. Accepted as their equal, the black sheep makes his fortune in dreadful Sodom. He would have lived happily were it not for the visit of his relative, a believer, my friend Lineu, along with two angels disguised as mortals, who warn him about the city's impending doom.

At the first cast meeting, the Hollywood Mexican revealed his concept for the punishment of Jehovah. A computer-generated meteor would enter the stratosphere, accelerating toward Earth, until it collided with the pagan village. Miss Lot, unable to resist a peek, would end up as a salt statue. The mold had required the actress to spend hours submerged in a tub full of plaster. Lot and his daughters seek refuge in a cave, perpetuating the species via the supreme taboo that is incest. Lineu's Abraham would return to Sarah's arms and, by a miracle, would impregnate his octogenarian wife, giving origin to Isaac, the father of Jacob, the hero of ensuing episodes. Decades of dramaturgy with the Biblical seal of quality. The promise of permanent work. The young Mario Cardoso would have disdained the opportunity that at that moment had me rejoicing.

†

I'd spent the afternoon in the studio, intent on maintaining my dignity during the orgy that opened the first episode. Ripped dancer girls weaned on iron and protein supplements shook their silicon during the Dance of the Seven Veils. A Zulu drum marked the beat for the pagan ritual. I delighted in a bunch of grapes, afraid of losing the gold crown poorly secured on my left canine by the talentless makeup lady whom the producers had brought on. The migraine brought on by the *interlace* used to give my hair more length whipped my cranium like needles. It was the greatest challenge I faced in that role, that of lasting seven hours with a weave. They stuck my implanted mane, headache and all, in a hideous turban, glued a goatee on my chin, and there I went, Sinbad the Sailor, sucking down grapes as I massaged the thighs of a member of the sheikh's harem. The third-millennium Sheik of Agadir. I should have asked for more money.

The joy of having found employment didn't last until lunch. The dancers' cherry lipstick, the league of hammy elders, the dialogue riddled with the coarsest slang to bring the modern viewer closer to the olden days. It took the entire afternoon to complete the Dantesque ballet, but the worst was still to come. Two Ethiopian sentinels interrupted the bacchanal, dragging a would-be actress off by her shaved armpits. Tossed to the floor, she knelt, begging for clemency. I thought about how much I was making and gave it my best, demanding sexual favors in return for forgiving the debts of her father, a humble pastor, a poor Hebrew sentenced to death. I gave a histrionic clap, the entire court let out an evil laugh, and the daughter of the condemned man was tossed outside by servants. Since the aspiring actress's tears stubbornly refused to appear, she started kicking her legs. Whatever, the chick was terrible even on her back. The camera reinforced Lot's interest for the disgraced Hebrew girl, the director yelled *Wrap!* and our interminable day came to an end.

I walked in the door dead tired. The smell of food wafted through the air. Home. My acting gifts could still earn a decent living for those who depended on me. I doused my hands in moisturizer, massaged out the gnarls left by the hairpiece, snuck a cigarette, got into my robe, and curled up on the couch, playing husband to my senile mother. Carine, tucked in the armchair to my left, was wearing an obscene pair of shorts and twisting every which way as she trimmed the cuticles of her toes. I relaxed, lulled by the suffering of others on the TV news. The telephone rang. It was Milena. She needed to see me, urgently, that very night, if possible.

We agreed to meet at Gomes's office, he would be there too.

I left the house in a hurry, going back over the last two years, trying to understand where I'd gone wrong. The building was entirely dark, a doorman was watching the end of the Wednesday night soccer match on a small black-and-white television. Without delay, he indicated the elevator to the eighth floor. I headed to Room 801, the last room on the right; the door was open. Milena and Gomes were waiting for me in the presidential suite, he was smoking a cigarette and looking less than confident. *Have a seat, Mario*, he ordered. The two of them exchanged glances, unsure who should speak first. Milena insisted that the accountant explain the situation. Gomes exhaled in a long sigh and offered me a cigarette. I accepted. That was how the opera began.

You know I like you a great deal, Mario, that I've always sought to keep your life on the right track, he said, pausing. I mentioned the late hour and asked him to skip the preamble. During the last month, Gomes had personally traveled to Brasília, he had contacts inside the Ministry of Culture and access to proceedings as they were developing. There was some suspicion over three hefty receipts, which amounted to a third of the *Lear* budget. A river of money that they had no way to account for. I inquired about the origin of this sum. *When I signed on to the project*, Milena said, taking the conversation from there, *Gomes explained to me just how important this production was to you*. Our little chat had gotten off to a bad start: was she suggesting that it was all my fault? Gomes noted my irritation and cut in, walking us through my professional crisis. He spoke of missteps, of the fear I'd shown at losing my TV contract, reminded me of the delicate situation hundreds of colleagues were facing. *Lear was more than a play, Mario, you were turning over a new leaf*. I reminded them that I had a shoot early the next morning and asked them once again to be direct. *The sponsor had demanded a risky guarantee*, Milena explained, clarifying that she had consulted Gomes before accepting any conditions. *Mota*, she said. I asked what Mota had to do with anything. *He threw all his weight behind the project to get it approved*, the producer continued, *he defended us before the board, suggested the Sponsor's Night in São Paulo.* Gomes fleshed out the narrative: *But these things come at a price, you know. No,* I responded, *I don't know. Mota saw himself as part of the project,* Milena continued, *but the law doesn't recognize this sort of commitment. Yes,* I said, *I'm not his boss, Mota receives a salary, the money's there to support culture.* Gomes cut me off, he was taciturn, *Not only. . . . Not only what?* I responded. Gomes was clear. *He was being paid off the books.*

I went mute. From the money raised, thirty percent ended up in the dandy's pockets, paid in cash, via Milena's cousin. *And there were no receipts?* I inquired. *Right, Mario, that's more or less it, all in cash, no receipts,* Gomes concluded. Behind his smug demeanor, that prick Mota was a carbon copy of the sort of swindlers you find everywhere, a vile broker feeding off the federal purse. He had his fee, the gatekeeper's commission. That's how things were, that's how they'd always been, it was infantile silliness on my part to think the theater wouldn't be susceptible to these tricks. I looked around at Gomes's sleepy office and remembered that gateway to hell where Mota had welcomed us. Raymundo Colares on the wall, the designer desk chair, the scent of a luxury goods store; the Ligia, Helio, and Guignards in the bastard's personal collection. Of course such spoils weren't the fruit of Mota's sweat. I sat there wondering which artwork he must have snatched up with my failed production. The crematory stench of that decrepit building climbed up my nostrils. My stomach seized with nausea. *It was no easy task,* Gomes conceded, *to make Mota disappear in the accounting reports.*

Without my knowledge, the dynamic duo had used the enterprise that bore my name to cook the books, hoarding receipts for tiny expenses like taxis, food, equipment rentals that never happened, without ever managing to make Mota's healthy cut disappear. *It was a lot of money*, Gomes said wistfully. The initial plan was to lower the sum over the course of the run, which would have been possible if we'd honored the national tour. Shakespeare in the North, the Northeast, this would bring tears to the Ministry's eyes and would also have given them the chance to doctor invoices from hotels, restaurants, light and sound rentals. *But then you came with that cackle of yours, Mario, one big jeering grin, the run was suspended, and that was the end of the whole scheme*, Gomes complained. When it became impossible to stall the rendering of accounts, the two of them agreed, together, to falsify three invoices, issued under the vague term of general expenses, and forwarded them to Brasília. *The Ministry didn't buy it*, Gomes admitted.

I suggested they seek out Mota, but Milena argued he might interpret it as blackmail and that would place us in a delicate situation with a major corporation. *We would put her cousin's job at risk; we would never again have access to any sort of sponsorship*, Gomes continued, *I know people in the same situation, you can end up a pariah if you sound the alarm*. To avoid a public scandal, it was necessary to return the money, with a fine, interest, and quietly assume fault. *How much?* I asked. *A great deal*, the accountant acknowledged, as he scribbled the sum on a scrap of paper. I unfolded it. I counted the succession of zeros that followed a number I didn't deign to look at.

I recoiled in my chair. That old shortness of breath. Milena ran to my aid and dragged me to the window. I looked down, the sidewalk beckoning me. *To sleep! Perchance to dream.* A cup of sugar water convinced me to put off suicide, I went back to the chair and broke down, defeated. The responsibility fell to me, Gomes couldn't guarantee a thing, I should have learned that a long time before, during *Razor to the Flesh*. An actor like Paulo Autran would never have done that, but I was no Paulo. Perhaps I'd even have agreed to all their dirty tricks, had I known from the beginning, so blind was I with Shakespeare, *Lear*, and Stein.

Gomes insisted on whispering something into my ear, but I didn't listen. He repeated that he would never abandon me, he liked me, that was his solemn promise. My eyes locked on his mouth, that giant, fat frog mouth, its yellow teeth, exuding bad breath. That snout was saying something to me. *A commercial ... I know ...* he'd found a campaign for me ... *nice, Gomes, nice.* When they realized what a disaster everything was, he and Milena set about dredging up the ad. A year long, they said, national television, billboards, bus boards. *This is big, Mario, even more so now that you're back to doing soaps! But what is the commercial for?* I asked. The two of them traded wary looks. *It's a surprise,* the accountant pivoted, *and it's not even you, Mario, it's Lear!* Milena—it was always Milena—knew an ad guy in São Paulo in charge of the account for an important advertiser. The agent incarnate, she'd sold the idea of using the monarch. *You don't even need to get permission from anyone,* the producer added, *Shakespeare's in the public domain!* They were still working on the concept, but we were talking big money, they assured me. If it didn't cover everything, it would cover part. *I'd never leave you hanging out to dry*, Gomes said, and gave me a hug.

Milena put me in a taxi. I was so confused that I thanked her for her kindness. As I was passing by Flamengo Park, I thought about John Gielgud, who ended up in that shitshow *Lost Horizon* thanks to an accountant. The actor discovered he hadn't paid taxes for three years, after the fucker had hit the road. He'd bought a mansion on the outskirts of London, was getting ready to retire, counted the number of empty seats at matinee showings. He suspected he would live a long time, as in fact he did. To avoid bankruptcy, he ended up in a monk's clothes, drowning in plush, burning up in a California desert while a machine launched torrents of foam at him to simulate Nepalese blizzards. Gielgud had made it. I would make it, too.

†

Carine and Maria Amélia slept on the living room sofa, the television still on. I left the two of them there and went to lie down in the company of my insomnia. When the clock struck seven, I cooled my head in a cold shower, numbed myself with painkillers, and went to work. I couldn't execute. I stumbled over my lines and forgot the script, barely maintaining control over my lips limp from barbiturates. I couldn't keep my mind off that fucker Mota, that dinosaur Gomes, and Milena Jovic.

The foul actress was brought to the villain's bedroom. I struggled, as I'd done the day before. Under my command, two slaves tore her vestments from her, leaving her lying on the floor with minimal clothing. It was my role to go over to the girl, lustfully pull her to me, bring my lips close to hers and demand a kiss. She would rebuff me and then I would displace her jaw, true to the melodrama's chauvinist cliché. As I stepped forward, shame caught up with me. I could only stoop so low. I halted before the girl, she turned to me and gasped, anticipating the blow. I stopped the scene, claiming I couldn't understand the character's rationale. The director, already annoyed by my paycheck, stared at me, stupefied. *Your character's rationale?* he exclaimed. *What's his motivation to treat her this way?* I continued. *His motivation*, he responded, *is to do what the script says, to honor his contract, to earn his salary, to say his lines, it's to not create problems one hour before we conclude a day with seven scenes still to go on his account; it's giving thanks to God he got this job without needing to beg for money in that shit theater you do; is that enough of a motivation for you?* I backed down, livid. *Roll the tape!* the director bellowed. I thought it prudent not to argue, I grabbed the girl, waited for her to rebuff me, and then took my palm to her face. Sprawled on the floor, the actress shot me a hurt look; she'd realized it was me, Mario, and not Lot, who had smacked her. A credible tear ran down her red face and I thought back to Marta. Marta, who left me after a smack across the face. Marta, whom I lived with for fifteen years and thanks to whom I became the man of means I am today.

ACCUSTOMED TO THE INDIGENCE of the stage, I rang the doorbell to the cinema mansion where the first read-through of the script of *Devil to Pay in the Backlands* would be performed. A uniformed employee opened the heavy wooden gate and I walked up the driveway toward the giant glass house encrusted with Joá stone. When I reached the main room, the director welcomed me with great enthusiasm, and next to him was the hostess, a knockout brunette wearing perfume and an Afghan kaftan.

Bento Peixoto had seen *Uncle Vanya* and had the intuition that I could be his Riobaldo. After Vado, he was certain of it. Only in me, he said reassuringly, had he found the mix of sensitivity and brutality that could account for the professor turned outlaw. My lack of onscreen experience hadn't scared him off, on the contrary, he dreamed of unknown faces and eyed me as though he'd discovered hidden treasure. I accepted the caipirinha and headed out to the balcony. Without visible support beams to mar the beauty of the architecture, the stage extended out toward the blue precipice of the Atlantic. I fought off my fear of heights and sat with my back to the view. The truth is I couldn't even remember why I was there, so thrown off was I by the opulent surroundings.

Other arts could be pure, it cost them nothing to be so; but cinema, no matter how marginal, carried the weight of its industry. Every director dealt with limited resources, especially money. So an unusual alliance was formed between movie producers and the moneyed elite desirous of purging their boredom through others' genius. A fair trade. The costly cans of film captured for posterity the wildest artistic delusions, while at the same opening doors for the intellectual class to the illustrious pack filling their pockets thanks to the Economic Miracle.

Vivi d'Aleçon had been born in southern Bahia; the off-spring of a traditional landowning family, she was educated at an all-girls school in frigid Switzerland, which she left to circle through that so-called Elizabeth Arden ambassadorial circuit. Between stays at the Côte d'Azur and the Amalfi Coast, she became friend and lover to Europe's crème de la crème, having frequented the legendary refuge of the Rolling Stones on the French Riviera during the band's forced exile due to a tax imbroglio. She emerged unscathed from her family's bankruptcy thanks to her liaison with an heir to the Aleçon group, which controlled a healthy chunk of the French GDP. Vivi saved him from heroin, though she consumed cocaine the way others sniff glue. Her husband spent most of his time in Paris while she flaneured from here to there to avoid the torturous winter. *I detest skiing*, she said, adding that her incompatibility with the sport had nearly led to divorce. Then she laughed, slurping her vodka through a tiny straw. She was devastating, Vivi was. I stood there, outside of myself, somewhere between drunk and hypnotized, basking in the upscale lasciviousness of that classy fox.

Bento Peixoto was different from the voluptuous minx in every way, which must have been what brought them to be so close, in addition to the fact that both hailed from the Northeast. The director had the air about him of a migrant fresh off the truck. His country-boy haircut, the short shirt barely buttoned across his flat belly, and his handmade leather sandals served as decoration for his puny frame and giant head, from which citations of Graciliano Ramos and João Cabral, poems by Drummond, and entire passages of Rosa sprang forth. He saw Glauber Rocha as his mirror image, Bento himself sought such comparisons. He'd met Vivi at Cannes, where he'd gone, along with a delegation of the defunct Embrafilme, to scrounge up subsidies for his ambitious project. He'd directed four shorts that had won awards at second-tier festivals and one full-length feature not entirely lacking in merit, and an adaptation of *Antigone*, set in the dungeons of the secret police, which hadn't survived the censors' pen. An audacious fellow, he'd decided to take on Guimarães Rosa's masterpiece.

Cannes coincided with the Formula 1 racing championship in Monaco. The jet-setter crowd's agenda included watching the race and then attending the galas of the films selected for the competition for food and drink. Vivi offered up highly coveted parties for the Al Capones of both industries at the villa she rented in the Cap d'Antibes. It was at one of these receptions that Bento, who hailed from Pernambuco and was endowed with felicity of phrase, convinced her to become co-producer of his mad venture. Vivi saw in the director the chance to give meaning to her annual stay in the tropics, and mutual interest sealed the deal that had brought us there, that evening, on the veranda designed by Zanine Caldas, the Bahian visionary and architectural rage for every socialite in the 1970s.

The urgency of making *Devil to Pay* assailed the director like fever. The cat couldn't contain himself, ignoring commas, faithful only to the exclamation point. The film, he insisted, would appeal to fans of both American Westerns and *Cahiers du Cinema*. At some point, I had the impression he was using us to fine-tune his acceptance speech, the Palme d'Or already in hand. Cocaine, the finest, consumed in homeopathic doses by the three of us that afternoon, kept the luster on his palaver. To prove that the project was legit, he laid out his plan of action. Vivi would open her farm on the border of Bahia and Minas Gerais to us, along with her grunts, the livestock, and some horses. Part of the resources would come from Embrafilme, and the rest from the socialite's contacts. We would have a month-long immersion on the property before filming began. The role of Diadorim had not yet been settled, but a novice actress with two green spotlights for eyes, the revelation of the latest Gramado festival, was the heavy favorite.

I was surprised by the size of the script, an encyclopedia twice as large as the original novel, but I didn't mind, I was already convinced. Vivi, the veranda, Cannes, Monaco and Formula 1, the red carpet, Mick and Keith, the snow, Bahia, Zanine, Joatinga Beach and Cap d'Antibes; no more of the Campos's huts, the dirty hippies on Ipanema, the stench of

Lapa, or the insanity of Raquel. Goodbye Plínio, goodbye Chekhov, au revoir Fidel and Che. Black God, White Devil in the Land of Rosa, the *Cahiers* would see. The one with the Palme in hand, then, was me. Vivi uncorked the champagne and we toasted to the afternoon. We opened the script to page one as the last ray of sunshine disappeared behind the horizon.

Four hours later, we still hadn't made it to page ten of the Passion of Bento Peixoto. The genius had scripted the novel paragraph by paragraph. And if that weren't enough, the combination of Stolichnaya, Veuve Clicquot, and happy dust deadened my tongue and locked my jaw. It became impossible to continue with the quickly unraveling reading.

> *Let me explain, sir: when the devil reigns in a man, in the squidges of a man—either he's a ruined man, or a foeful one.*

The devil, the devil, the devil. . . .

> *The devil in the streets, in the middle of the duster. . . .*

I jammed up. The sea, just outside, had transformed into a black abyss. The night wind howling through the open windows, the house enveloped in macabre shadows and the scum from the sea air on the furniture. The taste of zinc in my cotton mouth, which refused to articulate what was written. The crash. My blood pressure dropped and beads of sweat were released from my pores. Accustomed to the letdown, Vivi decreed the end of the night. *It's genius*, she said, *genius, genius, genius!* Then she put

Serge Gainsbourg on the turntable. *La décadanse*. I fumbled my way to the half-bath and tried to focus on the toilet bowl, but couldn't. I cleaned the lid with the flower-print toilet paper, washed my face, drank water from the faucet, and went back to face the end of the party.

Vivi was waiting for me. *Bento just left*, she said, *he's beguiled by you.* I paused awkwardly. *Just kidding*, she laughed, *I asked him to leave, I'm also beguiled.* She began to sway her way toward me, dragging her open-toe sandals while she lip-synced Birkin. *If I can barely control my tongue, imagine the rest!* I thought to myself. But I worried that a no would make me lose Riobaldo; how had I gotten to this point? Vivi was already inches from my mouth, when I decided to put an end to the suspense with a clumsy kiss. She laughed and dragged me outside. She had class, that Vivi. She'd noticed the state I was in and hadn't insisted on going further. We lay down on the lawn chairs and looked to the sky. The breeze, there outside, was refreshing. No, it had nothing to do with the breeze, it was I who had calmed down. My queasiness passed and I sat there in silence. We remained there for one, two hours, without saying a word. How rare it is, I thought, to sit quietly next to someone. Both of us were tired of Bento's yapping and his bloated script. Poetry was made to be read alone, of that I was certain. What imbecile vanity, wanting to stage it. I sat watching Vivi, her eyes fixed on the expanse.

Knowing how to make one at home, that was the woman's gift. And there was nothing trite or vulgar about it. There was a void in her, which was filled with zeal. Vivi had saved me, she must have done the same with her husband, I mused, and with

Bento, in Cap d'Antibes. We remained silent until the sunrise. When the sun grew hot, we looked to one another, new old friends. I asked her name. *Vilma*, she said. *Vilma*, I repeated. Then she led me to breakfast, set by who knows whom, on the dining room table made from a tree stump. I took a bite of the tiny croissant and dared to ask why she'd got involved in the film. *There's about as much of a script as there is modesty in Bento*, I reasoned. *I have my farm*, Vivi answered sincerely, *the means, the horses, the men, no one ever asked me before, only him, so why not?* I had no response. *That's the extent of my ambitions, and yours?* she continued. It took me a while to respond, I didn't want to lie. *I'm tired of the theater*, I confessed, but it wasn't only that. *Riobaldo is my dream*, I replied. *A strange thing to covet*, she observed, before going on to say that it would be great to have me in Bahia, to hear Rosa aloud, watch the horse stampedes. *This, for me, is already worth the risk*, she explained. She was right, the rest is silence, the rest nobody knows. *I accept*, I said, *for you, for Rosa, for Minas Gerais*. The servant girl alerted me that a driver was standing by for me. Before we said goodbye, Vivi leaned against the window of the Galaxy and confided that she'd like to introduce me to a friend of hers. *I don't know if you'll like her, but Marta sure is going to like you.*

It was the first time I'd heard the name of the woman who would become my wife.

I HAD BEEN ROOMING at the farmworkers' villa for three weeks. I refused to stay at the main house, I needed to adapt to the routine of the farmhands. I would set out for the cattle drives before sunrise, settling into the tough routine and their strange, truncated way of speaking that Rosa had translated into literature. A terrible horseman, I struggled to get a handle on the reins. They'd brought out a wild stallion whose back was taller than my scalp. I mounted him, trembling, with the help of a stool. The devil lowered his ears and bucked his head. I failed this test. The adrenaline kicked in, my eyes shot out, the beast could smell the fear on me and bounded into a hard trot. Thrashing around in the saddle, I let loose a *whoooa*, in an effort to tame the steed. My voice irritated the beast, and what was already trouble at a trot worsened at a brisk gallop. The fiend stiffened his jaw, stretched his neck, and turned on the turbines. My body lurched backward, I flailed around like an inflatable punching bag, and the equine began circling the paddock. Terrified, I spotted a tree trunk ahead. I didn't try to tame the animal, I clung to its mane and Bucephalus took an athletic leap, finishing with a backward kick that ejected me from my seat. When I came to my senses, I was eating dirt, my open mouth turned downward. I coughed up what I could. The grunt crew was cracking up, delirious with the asthmatic heart-throb sprawled out in the pasture, spitting up sand. Riobaldo required me to prove myself as a man, perhaps I wasn't up to it. I faced my dishonor with a chuckle and asked them to give me a gelding. When they took me to the corral, I caught sight of a dwarf horse eating from a trough, hidden between its full-grown parents. I asked them to saddle him up. The foreman didn't hide his disappointment, but between appearing to be something and not being it, I preferred deception. *Yes, that's the one*, I insisted. Bareta was a sad little thing. Dusky, thin, tiny, and resigned, he agreed to bear the burden. My feet, dangling outside the stirrups, nearly touched the ground. But Bareta, though gentle, was obstinate, ran at a smooth gallop, and didn't like to be left behind. The perfect match for a cowardly city slicker. Depending on the angle, we looked like a centaur in profile and I felt calm enough to focus on my lines.

Dora Franco, the novice with two green spotlights for eyes, preferred the comfort of the main house but soon changed her mind due to Bento's siege. The man from Pernambuco had gone mad for the girl. She was pretty, Dora, slender, petite, strong, without much in the chest, and hard muscles like some androgynous angel.

I was savoring a goat-meat stew in front of the bonfire when she showed up suitcase and all. *Diadorim won't be lying down on a bed of feathers*, she said, and scooped some stew from the pan. The problem wasn't the bed, it was Bento. We got on immediately, as partners, without any attraction to muddle our roles. I'd already been vaccinated by Raquel. Bento, no—he'd been battling an acute case of passionitus ever since he laid eyes on Dora. He'd spend the days planning how to film the final scene, in which Diadorim's true sex is revealed. He spent all day dreaming of the dolly, or perhaps a crane, that would move from a mega-close-up on the mythic pussy and climb to the skies. Bento closed in on her like an old goat. The resulting discomfort helped her find the gravitas suited to the girl disguised as a hired gun, and the reprieve of our complicity established the tie between Riobaldo and the woman, or man, he loved.

On the twentieth day of our adaptation to the country, a jet swept low over the farm, the foreman appeared fresh from the shower and informed us that the mistress of the house had just landed. I finished rounding up the cattle and returned that afternoon, where I was to be received by the patroness in the main house. We left Riobaldo and Diadorim on the set and wore our normal attire. Dora's skirt didn't look right to me somehow and she looked down her nose at my suit. Vivi embraced me, filled with pride, and stroked my waxen beard, which I'd let grow since accepting the role. She spoke of the anxiety that had overtaken her during the trip. The director closed in on the young actress, who shot me an exasperated look. To Dora, the devil in the backlands looked just like Bento. Vivi took note. As we were finishing our toast, I watched as, from the end of the hallway, a svelte figure with black hair and an elegant stride came toward us. The hostess flashed a seductive smile and introduced me to Marta. I blushed. We both blushed. The blood ran down through my pants, she lowered her gaze, and Cupid released a sigh of satisfaction, as though his work were done. Despite the difference in age, the two women were great friends. Vivi, who had never wanted to have children, had adopted the young woman, the daughter of an influential lawyer in Salvador, as her protégée. Marta was a sharp-witted beauty, with a diploma from Oxford. She'd studied English literature but still hadn't found her calling. *She's got time*, Vivi exclaimed, and sat us next to one another at the table so as not to leave things to chance. There was no need. I tripped over the rug as I pulled the chair out for Marta and stuttered over my first few words. We ate our food shyly, without paying much attention to Bento and his theories, while he spewed erudition to impress Dora. Vivi was enjoying herself with the two opposing couples. A courtesan, she evoked Eros. *A great god*, she said.

Marta had had innumerable suitors. Fancy lads, with first and last names, but boredom always frustrated these romances in the end. Her sweetness was only a first impression. On the outside, a thoroughbred princess, inside, as disturbed and unruly as Helena. Helena. Raquel. It was the memory of Raquel in the skin of the Russian woman that had made me lose my voice. It was the want of the object of my suicidal passion, whom I'd fallen for on the stage and who had vanished to reappear as Plínio's she-devil. I still suffered from the loss. Marta's appearance at the farm, in surroundings so much like Vanya's dacha, and her sardonic smile made me believe that I could relive it all. A delusion, I knew. Uncontrollable. I never loved anyone again, I said, because Marta existed only in Raquel's shadow. I was overtaken by romantic sentiments that, until then, had been unknown to me. I longed to be someone else so that I could be worthy of her. I longed to be Astrov. I sensed there was an entire future ahead of us, but this certainty came crashing down when I remembered the hole I called a home, the taxi that took me to the theater to the bars where I'd go drinking. It was there, in the dining room of the hundred-year-old farm belonging to Vivi d'Aleçon, that I chose the future that would tear me from the commie trattorias, my madness for kamikaze actresses, the filth of the rehearsal rooms, and the bohemian thrill of the Fiorentina. At that moment, I started to become the person I am today, a lazy actor in league with bloodsuckers raiding the national treasury. My mistake was to invest myself in the Bourgeois Gentleman, when Marta wanted Riobaldo. That's why I angrily smacked that wannabe actress in the Biblical soap and why I blamed my ex-wife for every bad thing that ever happened to me. I wanted to repeat the gesture that, one day, had torn us apart. It wasn't fair, I know, but nonetheless it felt good to place the blame on her.

*　　*　　*

The blow to the jaw that put an end to our marriage cracked against my wife's delicate face. Vado, Plínio's sleazeball invention, had never entirely left me. Just like the second-rate actress, Marta's eyes grew wide, full of fear. A slow tear traced a line to her chin and dropped to the floor. She rose to her feet and composed herself, then we faced each other for a long minute, enemies. I thought about asking her forgiveness, but there was no more time and nothing more to say. That was the end. Marta calmly wiped her face, walked to the bedroom, grabbed a handful of clothes, tossed them in a suitcase, and left. We never spoke again. Years later, I learned that she had married a well-to-do businessman, was happy, had become pregnant, and left Brazil.

When we met each other, at Vivi's farm, I sensed the gulf between my middle-class upbringing and her upper-class roots. The blessed fruit of a powerful clan from Bahia, she'd grown up on the family fiefdom, planted on the peak of a hill in Salvador, from which one could glimpse all three hundred and sixty-five churches in the capital city. The fortune of the Teles family dated back to the colonial era, rooted in livestock, sugarcane, and cacao. The family's descendants married among themselves or their equals. The rare intruders overcame this barrier only after a Herculean effort to play to type. Which was not my case. I remained a plebe, successful, but a plebe, incapable of breaking into the upper echelons. Marta sought to be a woman of her time, choosing for herself a fate different from that of all the aunts, mothers, sisters, and nieces, all molded to marry well. She had friends among the counterculture crowd and was hooked by the quintessential-Rio-man-cum-mercenary-Riobaldo. An actor. A thousand men in one—that was the fantasy that won her over.

*　　*　　*

The *Devil in the Backlands* that brought us together was over after four weeks of filming. Bento Peixoto's genius complex was the whirlwind that dragged him into the inferno. There was no room for ordinary plans, every scene brought with it the weight of posterity. The first day of filming was spent on a tracking shot that started with stumpy little Bareta's hooves and ended with a close-up of my sweaty brow. *Sell your own soul . . . Shamfull inventation! And the soul, what is it. The soul has to be the most inwardly thing*, I would say. Dora Diadorim would come on horseback, from behind me, the camera's focus would shift to her face, and we would set off like lightning. But Bareta refused to stop on his marks, and so did Dora's steed. The animals' stubbornness and the actors' equestrian amateurism spoiled the framing. We tried all morning without success. Of the three sequences that were to be filmed that day, we managed only two shots from the first, which we repeated the next day and the next. We burned through film canisters like matches. After four weeks, we realized that we would never make it to the end. Not only had we made little progress, the backing money didn't come through as promised. Vivi failed to attract investors and Embrafilme would disburse a second installment only once we'd filmed half the movie. Coming back from a day off just as we were completing a month of shooting, Bento announced he would be tackling the final scene. He was in low spirits, he'd laid off part of the team, absorbed the workload, and lost weight. He'd lost his prior eloquence and turned to drinking, alone, living in the shadows of the main room of the farmhouse. The only thing still motivating him was a single desire, that of rolling the sequence in which Diadorim, lifeless and naked, is revealed to be a woman. Aware that he lacked the means to continue, Bento focused his energies on this farewell. He had to find a way to give meaning to it all.

The crane was mounted inside the crammed hut. A contraption some twenty-five feet high, dragged along a suspended track. We spent the morning putting this piece of rudimentary engineering in place. The tiles on the house's roof were taken down, the mud floor made level, the track elevated along a runway of slats, screws, and wedges. Bento hurled insults at the team, acting as if everyone but he were to blame. He made a point of sitting on the crane, together with the photographer and the focus technician, but there wasn't room for all three. He opted to dispense with the former and handle the camera himself. Faced with the impossibility of his fantasy of possessing Dora, he would penetrate her with the lens. He'd gone mad. He ordered everyone off the set. The only ones left were me, him, and Dora, who walked on set draped in a robe. Bento scurried to remove it, but the young woman stopped him. She loosened the knot herself before lying down on the table, mechanically, oozing frigidity to tame the filmmaker's lechery. Seeing her naked atop the wood, Bento disappeared for a moment, taking slow breaths, frozen in place. I tried to rouse him, asking him to go over the mise-en-scène one more time. Bento thoughtlessly pointed to a corner, grunting at me to remain still, and called the team together. The crew assumed their posts, but their discomfort was clear. Bento stared at Dora with such lust that we feared we were about to witness rape.

I felt more pity for him than for her, for the pathetic figure Bento Peixoto had become. He climbed atop the crane, the grips set their counterweights on the opposite side to stabilize the arm and lifted him into the air. He ordered them to back it down and lower the camera toward Dora's pubis. *Beautiful . . . beautiful!* he exclaimed, and then cried *Action!* We ran through the scene. Dora played dead, I drew close to the table, the lens following her slender body until it settled on my face; I made the sign of the cross and the steel arm began its ascent. *Slower! Slower, goddammit!* the maestro demanded. The crane's base reached the end of the track and the platform stretched to the ceiling. I was getting ready to begin my lament when the choreography was interrupted by the assistant's warning voice. THE CROSSBEAM! he cried. An error in calculus had pushed the jib against what was left of the hovel's roof. They tried to put the brakes on, but inertia propelled it higher and Bento's head crashed against the roof. We heard a sharp knock. We all looked up to find the director groggy, held up by the focus puller, yards from the ground. *Lower it! Lower it!* they yelled. Bento was laid out on the floor, bleeding. Dora ran to cover herself, we all gave the day up for lost but the *condottiere* emerged from his daze, arose like a man possessed, and pounced on the key grip, accusing him of purposely inflicting injury. We separated the two men, a break was suggested to calm the nerves, but Bento wanted to shoot. Seeing that Dora had left the table and dressed once again, he headed straight toward the actress and tore off her robe. *Lie down!* he ordered, *I didn't tell anyone to leave their positions*. The photographer offered to operate the lens, but Bento, wiping the blood from his forehead, barred him with a shove. We started from scratch. A close-up on the pussy, my livid face, sign of the cross, the camera panning out, and once again, the crossbeam jammed it. A break for coffee, some tweaking, nails, wedges, hammering. Dora nude once again, me livid, the cross, Bento with his head flush against the lens, out of focus. *From the beginning!* The angle was wrong, my body covering up Diadorim's crotch. *First position!* The wheels locked against the improvised track. *Again!* Without anyone noticing, the repetition had taken a toll on the precarious structure, where two men and an iron seesaw weighing more than four hundred pounds kept each other in check. The mud floor had given way, throwing off the dolly, but Bento wouldn't authorize a break so we could reinforce the base. It was the twenty-eighth time we tried to execute his plan. After so much up and down, the director threw off his safety belt. Now he swung freely in space, doling out commands and curses. Possessed, he decided to risk it. *Let's roll*, he roared, *it'll all come together!* I looked at Dora's body and thought of Raquel, my warped, imperfect love. The memory had me mourning all over again and I felt a pang in my heart. Dora held her breath, I assumed position, livid, Bento jammed the camera between her legs and cried *Action*. As if by magic, everyone performed their part in the orchestra to absolute perfection: the grips overcame their difficulty in dragging the jumbled mess along the warped track, my head didn't get in the way of Dora's privates, the focus didn't become soft, I made the sign of the cross, and when the camera hopped the girder, surpassing the roof tiles, Bento, bent over the viewfinder, was raised to the heavens. I howled like a rabid hound, picturing Raquel on the table; and as though God himself were lamenting Diadorim's death, a light rain began to fall at that exact moment. The tiny drops glimmered against the late afternoon light and the director exclaimed *Beautiful! Beautiful!* from on high. Bento let the camera roll until it beeped; then, he peeled his eyes from the lens and was swept away by a poignant teardrop. *That's cinema, goddammit!* he murmured to himself. *That's cinema!* Everyone applauded, embraced, the sequence was worth an entire film. That's when a thunderous crack, as though an elephant had broken a rib, put an end to our rejoicing. We looked around, startled. Another crack, followed by creaking wood. Without our noticing, the rain had soaked the earth, compromising the beast's foundations. *Run!* someone screamed. I snatched Dora by the arm and got out of there as fast as I could. The drumbeat of tragedy echoed at our backs. I looked behind me to see Bento, the focus technician, and the camera tumble to the ground. The rain kept the dust from rising, the crane plummeted in a straight line, taking what was left of the hovel with it. A terrifying silence followed. We waited until we heard a groan rise from the rubble. We ran to help. The focus technician was found next to the camera, strapped to the safety belt. Bento, tossed high above the ceiling beams, had landed awkwardly on the mud and straw ruins. He was inert, terrified, his breathing labored. The team formed a circle around him and I knelt down to help him. The foreman called a neighboring farm and asked them to send a puddle jumper as fast as they could. Bento looked up at Dora and called her My Diadorim. Dora remained expressionless. She found the director disgusting, even standing before his ragged body. He was taken away as night fell, strapped to a plywood plank that served as a makeshift stretcher. The focus technician went with him, walking on his own two legs, to be examined at a hospital in Salvador. He was carrying a film canister in his hands. The film, protected inside the camera, had survived the fall.

†

We rolled the raw footage from that afternoon in a private showing in the projection room of one of Vivi's friends. Joining Vivi were Dora, Marta, the photographer, and I. Bento remained hospitalized with several fractures and a head contusion, but without any risk of seizures. The lights dimmed, the lamp lit the screen, we watched the film lab's countdown, followed by the shot whose beauty it was impossible to deny. The sacred pussy, Dora's body, my lost gaze, the sign of the cross, my soul rising, the hovel with its roof undone, my howling voice, and the couple's solitude. Finally, the light rain falling in perspective, accentuating the depth of field. The filmmaker's last chimera. It was moving to see. And to think of what might have been.

What way out is there for an artist, I thought, *if not inner immolation?* Other professionals eat, drink, screw, have a good time, and even endure this slavery without suffering. I couldn't handle many more of these experiments, I wanted a job that would allow me to survive, that was it. I looked to Marta, that complete woman, sitting in the chair next to mine. Someone who didn't suffer from a split personality like Raquel; or preach about revolution, like Campos; who didn't have the certainties of Guria, much less the wild ambition of Bento. Marta, who was who she was, because of who she was, solid, rational, and she wanted to know if I was for real. We left to go to her apartment in Gávea. I asked her to lie down on the bed, like Diadorim. I ran my hands over her pale body, I held her hair, I wanted a way out. *Let's run away?* I asked. And she said yes.

†

Eight months later, we were flying to Cap d'Antibes. Vivi had convinced a Parisian film editor to edit the footage from *Devil to Pay in the Backlands*. She'd given him credit as co-director and the film, almost a documentary, was selected for a festival running in parallel to Cannes. The result was surprising. The Frenchman gave the work the title *Obsession*, editing a month's worth of material, preceded by hundreds of frustrated attempts. Bareta's hooves and my ear invading the frame, Dora's face out of focus, the horses who refused to stand in place; the unfinished cavalcades, the expanses of Minas, and the camps set up for the night. Finally, the thousand and one efforts to make the final scene work, interspersed with still photos. Bento reeling, head bloodied; Bento locking horns with the key grip, Bento tearing the robe from Dora's body; Bento climbing up and down the crane; the director's fall. His wounded body amid the rubble. And, just before the lights went out, the blessed take, Bento Peixoto's resurrection. *Hushed; very hushed is how we summon love: as in hushedness things summon us*. Serge Gainsbourg, at Vivi's request, underscored the narrative with passages from the novel in French; and I did the same, in Portuguese. Bento appeared at the showing, still strapped to a wheelchair. The commotion impeded him from exercising his typical logorrhea. He permitted himself only to cry, in light of the sincere applause he received from the audience; the road was winding, but he'd finally reached the place he'd dreamed of.

We completed the festival rounds. Dora showed her face on the French Riviera, but refused to accompany the rest of the procession. She felt bad, she didn't like lying, she hated the director. Bento didn't have the strength to stick to the schedule either. Marta and I took advantage of this postmortem to get to know each other better. Vivi made a point of my presence at the innumerable galas, press conferences, and events that followed Cannes. She wanted Bento's film and my romance with Marta to be a success. Without a livelihood, I had no way of keeping up with all the travel, but Vivi saw to this crisis with more-than-respectable remuneration for me to accompany *Obsession* on the European circuit. She included Marta in the entourage as a translator, which made it possible to continue our time together and have a relationship of equals. I saw Paris, Rome, Madrid, London, and Prague. I was happy in all of them.

At the end of the odyssey, after nearly a year far from Brazil, I dragged Marta to the garden in the palace where the closing ceremony of the Valladolid Festival was held. The Spanish smoked like machines in the closed space, and we fled the room to alleviate the burning in our eyes. We looked at one another as companions, knowing that eventually we would have to face the return to Brazil. *I've been invited to be part of a ten o'clock soap*, I said, *I think I should probably accept.* Marta agreed, she was tired of living on the road. I confessed my fear of losing her. *Things will be different in Rio*, I warned, *I'm not the same guy you've known until now, I sleep poorly, I eat poorly, and live much worse.* Marta kissed me, unworried about the uncertain future. She had also been making plans. She considered sending her CV to a university, perhaps lecturing, nothing concrete beyond her desire to take a chance on a life with me. *I admire you, Mario*, she said. She didn't mention love, and I didn't think anything of it. I should have. It wasn't this that brought us together but the desire to lose ourselves. I longed to be like her, and she, like me. We said goodbye to the first world in Madrid, we spent the night going from bar to bar, we danced and drank until sunrise. Later, we went to the hotel to screw and sleep. Intimate, the way a couple should be. We woke up a short time before our flight, jammed a year of life together into our suitcases, and embarked on a marriage that would last fifteen years.

†

Back in the furnace that was Guanabara Bay, I sent Jackson the contract for the dump in Ipanema that I had rented during my days in *Uncle Vanya*. He'd been seeing to the crap I'd left behind for months, in exchange for a safe landing in Rio's swanky Zona Sul. I'd rid myself of everything that no longer had any emotional value, memories of my teenage years, the T-shirts that a hippie friend had tie-dyed, the hash pipes from the wild days at the Ipanema; I kept a portrait of Raquel as Helena. The rest went straight to the trash. Jackson gave me a hug, thanked me for cleaning up, for the roof, and said he hoped we wouldn't lose touch. My partner had noted a change in me. My neat hair, my skin yellowed from the lack of sun, and, above all, the adult civility that I had acquired during my long stay in Europe. Jackson had found work in the choir of *Pippin*, the Bob Fosse musical imported from Broadway. He took home a miserable salary, had a place to lay his head, and didn't worry about what the next day would bring. He was the same Jackson I'd left there in Rio. I was not. The new, cultured Mario no longer fit in the musty one-bedroom with a stench of pot, sweat, and sex that would offend the noses of Marta's Gávea neighbors. Marta's apartment smelled of flowers, just like its owner. With a line of windows opening to the forest behind the building, it was typical to be visited by marmosets and toucans that came by to say hello as the sun rose.

†

Marta insisted on officializing our union with a dinner for my parents. Daughter- and mother-in-law spoke of music, art, and shared thoughts about Maria Amélia's professor routine in the Department of Literature. The diploma from Oxford had secured Marta an opening to teach foreign literature at Pontifícia Universidade Católica do Rio de Janeiro, two blocks from where we were living. So moved was he by his prodigal son, my father barely spoke a word. We walked to the veranda and lit a Gitanes I'd brought back from France. He coughed black smoke and preferred his old Menthols. Jorge Cardoso, choking up, revealed that he'd spent the last few years convinced that he'd lost me forever. Then he thanked me for cutting my mane and going back to taking showers.

A lover of Sinatra and MGM musicals, Jorge nurtured a healthy disgust for communists. Despite his liberal-democratic tendencies, he trusted that the military coup would free the country from the threat of becoming the next Cuba. Indifferent to the surveillance and torture imposed by the dictatorship, he had advanced, thanks to the Economic Miracle, to junior partner at an engineering firm. He would consider himself a happy man were it not for his disgust at seeing his only son join up with the lunatics that infested the planet. To him, the licentiousness of *Hair* was a greater threat than the armed resistance. At least the leftist militants had widely recognizable historical roots, embodied by Prestes, Jorge Amado, and Oscar Niemeyer. But there was no room for the theater in Jorge Cardoso's social order, and much less for the hippies wandering Leblon. For all these reasons, seeing me cohabitate—his word—with a decent woman, sleeping in a proper bed and eating my meals at a table touched him to the core. Me too, I must admit. To see, after a long period when we didn't speak, some sign of approval in my father's eyes brought me immense comfort. Marta was the medal I wore as proof of my maturity.

I prayed a lot for you, he said, unable to continue. He limited himself to placing his hand on my shoulder. *Life always finds a way for us*, he said in a choked whisper. Before returning to the living room, he told me how proud he was of me. Despite what I might think, he'd watched all my exploits onstage. It was my turn to lose my voice.

WERE HE STILL ALIVE, what would Jorge Cardoso think of his son now, running in a field in Jacarepaguá, dragging with him a fake beard, a turban, two imaginary daughters, and a wife, all dressed like it was *I Dream of Jeannie*? Would he still be proud of me? No, I don't think so.

Two more weeks and shooting for the biblical drama would be over. My only goal and encouragement was to make it out alive. A chroma key screen the size of a high-rise had been erected at the end of the meadow. There, the collision between a fiery meteor and Sodom would be applied in postproduction, in a computing miracle conceived by the Mexican imported from Hollywood. We repeated the scene to exhaustion; no acting was necessary. Thanks to our lack of physical conditioning, we panted at the right time, simulating panic rather than exhaustion. Though we performed our roles diligently, there was no creative angst, no flashes of genius from those involved, nothing that might recall the art house films of Bento Peixoto. New times. The one giving the orders offstage was the Holy Father of Special Effects. We, the cast, felt the mercy of a redemptive shadow each time we hit our marks, as I did better than Bareta, the miniature horse from *Devil in the Backlands*, who had come into the world without Lassie's talent. Mario Cardoso barked on cue and even helped the rest of the cast to find the right light. After the rocky start of shooting, I never again questioned my character's motivations, nor did I delay in performing my role. In return, I was treated like a star, which helped me to endure the dry routine.

Having agreed on a general plan, we attacked the day's second challenge, that of transforming Lot's wife into a salt sculpture. I kept myself from succumbing to my old side-splitting crack-up before the statue imitation of my clumsy colleague; and I hammed it up as much as I could, panto-miming horror, hiding my eyes behind my palms, shedding tears at the feet of the white statue. The workday ended, I crossed the field, admiring the paraphernalia of cameras, dollies, tracks, and reflectors scattered across my path. TV had become more sophisticated, a great deal more, in recent decades. What did I have to complain about? Parading around in a turban was nothing, compared with what I had been ready to do to my career. I climbed aboard the dressing-room bus, scratched the interlace on my head and removed my pointy little beard, careful not to aggravate the wounds on my chin, which had opened up after months of gluing and ungluing. I put my clothes on over my sweaty body and went to meet with Gomes in his office to sign the contract for the commercial that would free me from the proceedings at the Ministry of Culture.

I followed the Linha Amarela, the loop that circulated throughout the Rio suburbs. I marveled at the landscape dominated by houses, low-rise buildings, favelas and slums without vegetation. A heat wave strong enough to fry an egg on the asphalt was punishing the region, the air sweltering thanks to the dense Tijuca Forest, which acted as a barrier to the sea breeze, keeping the air from circulating. *The suburbs sure are ugly*, I thought. This wasn't always the case. In the seventies, when I began in television, Jacarepaguá, Engenho de Dentro, Del Castilho, Inhaúma, Pilares, and Bonsucesso still had something of the rural life, backyards with orchards, vegetable gardens, chickens, and dogs. But they'd paved over everything, the entire outlying suburbs; they'd cut the trees and transformed the simple lanes into bottlenecked two-way roads where the exhaust from buses stained buildings and city walls, casting a coat of soot over city squares where people once played cards, chess, and soccer. I was careful not to miss my exit. In the jumble of huts without water or sewage across Rio's impoverished communities, AK-47s abounded, trafficked along with baggies full of dust. *The people today have nothing of the idealism of my time*, I thought, *the poor sitting in chairs sprawled along the sidewalk*. This social inequality hadn't only destroyed the Tijuca of my childhood, it had taken over the neighboring communities, leveling the desolate landscape. The Linha Amarela was proof of this nightmare.

I pulled into a parking garage, removed my wristwatch, hid my wallet and cell phone in the inside pocket of my suit coat, taking the necessary precautions to avoid being mugged. I walked attentively, looking from side to side, toward the commercial building where Gomes was waiting for me. The homeless and grifters high on paint chips shared the sidewalk with those who still earned a living. The audience, what an abstraction. Who still went to the theater? Who cared about Shakespeare, Chekhov, Molière or Plínio? Who read Rosa? The street overrun with street vendors peddling plastic cell phones, nylon umbrellas, and Chinese junk. Globalization's fallen Babel.

I wound my way through, clinging to my pockets as though to life itself, eager to be clear of all that Paraguayan crap. That's when a swaying voice rose above the general pandemonium. *A, B, C . . . Baby, you and me girl. . . .* My eyes scoured the tents until I came upon a graying Afro and a face I knew, older now, hidden behind some fake designer sunglasses. *Three for five!* the guy cried, hoisting windproof lighters into the air. I stopped before this figure, who went mute, lowered his glasses, and looked at me, open-mouthed. Jackson, it was Jackson Five, my comrade from *Hair*, my brother from my younger days. *Mario . . . you son of a bitch!* he exclaimed. We clutched each other in a bear hug, two present-day shipwrecks, in middle of the crowd.

Jackson smelled like an armpit, he was gaunt, he'd aged, but hadn't lost his sly charm, the survivor's vibe he'd always exuded. Our embrace at an end, there wasn't much to say, it was clear that life hadn't smiled upon him the way it had me. *Yeah, Mario . . . it ain't easy, that's for sure*, he said with the sheepish grin of someone who hadn't got his due. *What about the theater?* I asked him. *It didn't work out*, he confessed, *I wasn't born for it, a handsome guy like you*. He ran his hand over my head. We laughed, ill at ease. I showed my disdain for fate, I showed him my middle-aged belly and receding hairline, told him about my failed *Lear. At least you still have hair*, I said, trying to cheer him up.

Jackson was already a grandfather, he'd had children early, which had forced him to leave the spotlight behind. He spoke with pride of the two families he'd raised, his nearly simultaneous marriages. He took care of everyone, twelve in all between wives, sons, brothers, nephews, and grandchildren. He lived in São Gonçalo, on the other side of the bridge, hustled in the city center, and ran like hell when the cops showed up. *I became a shower-time singer*, he joked, *but I can still hit the high notes.* To prove that his velvet voice remained intact, he sang *Ben, the two of us need look no more.* . . . *We both found what we were looking for* . . . I continued. . . . *With a friend to call my own* . . . *I'll never be alone* . . . and we finished together, locked in an embrace. *And you, my friend, will see.* . . . *You've got a friend in me.* . . . The neighboring street vendors, all Jackson's buddies, applauded, I was moved to find him there. To ward off the rush of emotion, Jackson told me how much he'd laughed at me in the soap, dressed up like a sheikh. The whole family knew about our friendship. *You were born to shine, Mario Cardoso!* he said prophetically, *and I to hustle!* I bought a pack of lighters and shoved a wad of cash into his hand. *Tonight we'll dine on filet mignon in your honor!* he said with joy. We said goodbye, promising to see each other again but knowing full well that wouldn't happen. Life separates people, the same way it separates us from ourselves.

I lit a cigarette with Jackson's Chinese lighter there on the sidewalk outside Gomes's door. It was a potent little torch, I was thinking I'd got quite a deal, but the piece of junk broke on the third light. I put it in my pocket, a souvenir. I said good morning to the doorman and headed up the stairs, the elevator was out of order. When I walked into his room, Gomes was smiling. *What's that all about?* I asked. *Luck!* he answered, telling me to relax.

Negotiations over the commercial lasted three long months. Milena and Gomes had joined forces, she in league with the São Paulo agency, he arm-twisting to close on a sum that would allow me to quit my debts and put the shameful episode behind me. For their efforts, each would receive 10 percent of the contract. I didn't haggle over the price. Of the remaining 80, 30 would be spent on taxes and 50 on the *Lear* shortfall. I wouldn't see a cent.

Aren't you pleased? Gomes inquired, *the whole proceeding is going to be shelved.* He was right, I was a lucky man, Jackson was proof of it. *If I were to lose my way*, I asked vaguely, *would you turn on me?* Gomes demanded I stop being a drama queen. He swore my problems ended right there, with that contract. I wanted to believe it. I initialed pages and pages without reading the clauses. I signed four copies allowing the use of my image nationwide for a year. Billboards, buses, print ads in magazines and newspapers, television commercials, electronic media, three ads for radio, life-size cardboard cutouts in supermarkets, not to mention launch events, with me going dressed as a king. *A full-on campaign, important stuff*, Gomes gloated. I shook the hand of my accountant, swearing to forget it. To get over it. If they wanted my kidney, I'd give it. Times had changed, I wasn't in any position to make demands. I was no young man and I no longer had the future ahead of me I'd once had.

WELL-RESTED, I woke up in the twin bed in the apartment in Gávea. Marta had already left for the university. Clean-shaven and showered, I went to meet the director of the first of many soaps to come. I disguised my anxiety with a blasé exterior, pretending I didn't give a damn whether I got a yes or no from the country's largest TV network. There was an irreconcilable antagonism, in my understanding, between art and business. But all it took was passing through the turnstile in the lobby to covet a job as a worker bee at the majestic factory. Entire sets were put up and taken down overnight. Fully equipped studios, separate rooms for makeup, costume fittings, and lounges where dozens of idols drank their coffees while practicing their lines. A legion of employees to give substance to something as fleeting as dramaturgy. To hell with others' prejudices, the accusation that the colossal network had been shored up to serve the interests of the regime. It was a state-funded monoculture, without any competition capable of overshadowing it, that was true, and it acted as the official organ of an authoritarian republic. On the other hand, a significant number of writers, actors, and directors who had survived political witch hunts had found shelter in those hallways. A not inconsiderable front, capable of producing relevant content. It was this restless wing that had shown interest in a promising actor like me. The station's position as absolute leader in viewership made this risk possible, and the fourth evening series, where I was about to find a job, was dedicated to discovering new ways of communicating. I was interested, of course, in the stable salary, which would allow me to split the bills with Marta; but I would have accepted, even for nothing, the role of Vicente in *The Year '15*, the Rachel de Queiroz novel about the devastating drought that befell the Northeast at the turn of the twentieth century. A rough riding cowboy and son of landowning gentry, Vicente would benefit from my experience as Riobaldo. Ready to tackle leading livestock and with a command of spurs, I dove right into the role that demanded no artistic concessions. Fortune had smiled upon me, and television, at that moment, offered everything I had ever dreamed of.

†

Vicente was an unprecedented hit. The success I'd known in the theater took on national proportions with the television. Odes from the critics, even those with the most reservations about the channel. Viewership climbed whenever I appeared on the screen. Love letters piled up in the casting department, women screamed my name outside the channel's doors. But Marta was special, her culture, her beauty, my trump card. Our marriage was going well, there were neither neuroses nor sickening passion. It would be a while before I crossed the line of disrespecting her, first in secret, then in the open. But recurring adultery wasn't the cause of our separation. It was the admiration that, one day in Spain, she had said she felt for me, and which slowly unraveled until there was nothing left. It was my role as rural henchman in a colonial-era soap, which had followed the fiasco of the tropical Hitchcock, a failed *Vertigo*. It was the whip I took to the mestiza girl. It was my fall as an actor that provoked Marta's disgust. Her disappointment with the actor. She had her affairs, too, things happen, we handled those well. But the daughter of Bahia royalty would never suffer a marriage to a third-rate comedian, a dime-a-dozen Tom, Dick, or Harry. Marta had loved Riobaldo, Vicente, Astrov, and event Vado, even Vado she'd loved. Or the old hypochondriac Argan, Molière's imaginary invalid, a role I'd accepted on her advice and which dragged legions out to the theater. The slave-driver José Dias, no, he was too much for Marta.

"I can't take your mediocrity anymore." That was the phrase I heard arriving home one day after a cast party for a recent soap, where I drank more than I should have and put up with the arrogance of the upstart heartthrob explaining to me that life existed outside television. *I can't take your mediocrity anymore*, that was the confession that earned her a whack across the cheek.

†

Fifteen years. Infinite changes, imperceptible changes, today, all compressed into an instant. It's impossible to add up all the moments that led me to the edge of the abyss. But I can point to the origin, the first sign of the deterioration that was to come.

The triumph that was *The Year '15* guaranteed me a three-year contract, a new and significant occurrence. My anxiety as an artist, the shots in the dark, the fear of what was to come were replaced by the comfort of serving a powerful employer. I was able, finally, to relax. Once I'd signed the boatload of clauses, initialed every page, I left the offices of the telecommunications giant radiant. I felt light, my feet barely touching the ground. It was a morning in May, the cold sun reminded me of Europe. Everything propitious and promising, the day called for celebration. I strolled with no particular destination, gazing at the display windows. A watch, perhaps . . . too pedestrian. I was looking for a symbolic object that could make my accomplishment real. That's when a vision came to me. On the opposite sidewalk, behind the glass of a luxury-goods vendor, a two-seat convertible, a near-faithful replica of the English MG TD, put an end to my searching. Nothing would supplant the MP Lafer, nothing would replace it. It had the engine of a VW Bug and a fiberglass body, but what did it matter, I thought, given the impeccable retro styling? I signed the payment plan, installments spread out over a year, because I could, my professional stability made it all possible.

In the garage, the beast finally mine, I turned the key, the low-horsepower engine purred, and I off I drove. I paraded through the city, zigzagged through the beaches, I drove the Flamengo Park circuit more than once before parking in front of the university where Marta gave classes. I meant to slay my wife with pride. The students formed a circle around the apparition, some asked for autographs, others ran their hands along the body; a nervy girl asked to get in next to me. I let her. I gave a juvenile chuckle despite my age. A thousand incarnations before that, when I was the same age as those kids, I had crammed into a pickup bed in service of waking the masses in the Pernambuco backlands. A dizzying ascent, I noted, crowned by a most glorious honorarium. Marta walked through the door. Discovering the cause of the commotion, she laughed, not sure whether to believe it. *Want a ride?* I asked matter-of-factly. She responded that she lived close by and was in the habit of going on foot. *I insist*, I answered as I politely dispatched the student settled in the passenger seat. Marta feigned jealousy and took her place. I wrapped her up in a kiss and the crowd roared. It was an event. I drove up Rua Marquês de São Vicente toward the tunnel that led to what was then the sandpit of Barra da Tijuca. My hand on Marta's thigh, I was in love with life, but above all with myself. We crossed the long stretch of beach, the sea air against our faces, hair fluttering in the wind. Reaching the remote beach of Recreio, we waited until the sun disappeared and screwed beneath the night sky, in the narrow space between the doors.

It became my habit to go cruising around in the MP. The sides of buses scratched to hell pulled up next to the convertible in the midst of bottlenecks and I pretended not to notice the little heads, squished inside the sardine can, flashing jealous looks. A pathetic sense of awe, I know, beyond my control. The new sports car required adjustments in its owner. I adopted a foulard around my neck and gradient Ray-Bans; I surrendered to the elegance of the vest sans blazer, adorned by a leonine haircut treated with expensive shampoo. Marta always chuckled. She had noted my metamorphosis without guessing that, one day, the monster would turn on her. I began frequenting Frenetic Dancing Days and, a while later, Régine's and the Hippo, gradually working my way up to Travolta-like moves on the dance floor. I became close to the upper-crust bohemian crowd, painters, journalists, filmmakers, and all the music stars. An ample amnesty buried the military dictatorship once and for all and political activism petered out to the beat of a sensual, intoxicating, dizzying hedonism.

†

This bind they call fame. It's impossible to see it that way, when it sings your praises and bats its eyelashes. My own came around at the height of my hormones and I relished it with the pure elation of youth. A full head of hair, nonexistent belly, firm muscles, and Homeric proportions. My height alone, a full head above the national average, was enough to make me stand out among the crowd. On TV, I doubled in size. I experienced a joy I'd not known up to then the first time I found myself surrounded by a legion of people I didn't know. It happened in a store in Ipanema, where I'd stopped to buy tennis shoes. The saleswoman trembled as she knelt down to adjust the shoelaces, giggling with her colleagues, who envied her chance to attend to the soap opera heartthrob. I was surrounded at the checkout, first by female employees, then by other clients. I spent more than an hour there, being flirted and fawned over. I related the events to Marta, seeking to disguise my delight. She laughed.

Should I be worried? she kidded. I responded, sincerely, that no one could stack up to Marta.

And no one could. But it was difficult to control. The one who didn't stack up was me.

Toward the end of *The Year '15*, a high-circulation men's magazine proposed a profile. The editor, a woman, had taken it upon herself to do the interview, a sign of prestige in journalistic circles. There would be four conversations with Consuelo Fontes, a blazing-hot brunette, who tagged along during shoots and was welcomed into my home for photos. For two weeks, we lived as though there were no difference in gender between us. I gave opinions on everything: politics, arts, men, women, left, right, drugs, love, and fidelity. It was the first time I spoke of myself in the third person, as though Mario were someone else. The heroic narrative overstimulated my vanity, way more than the throngs of anxious and wailing fans. The acid I'd dropped in Ipanema, the improv performances that ended in orgies, Raquel's suicide, the armed resistance in Pernambuco, Bento's accident, the film festivals, my romance with Marta; the "this is my life" at age thirty ended up convincing me that Mario Cardoso was, after all, a shining demigod, a Marvel superhero. Consuelo maintained her reporter's skepticism, but she started to open up, share her own opinions, and even talk about her own life without my asking. The day we had her to our apartment in Gávea, Marta noted our intimacy. We drank wine, the three of us, my wife laconic. Raised to be polite, she considered it in poor taste to share secrets and rebuffed efforts to include her in the interview. She finally agreed after

I insisted, saying I was proud of her, of the two of us. *I'm not a misanthrope*, I said ironically, citing Molière, whom she liked so much. Marta accepted but posed without smiling and made no secret of her discomfort at Consuelo's skillful snooping. With her beauty queen smile, the editor made her way to the subject of jealousy, she wanted to know if Marta was possessive. *I'm not here to talk about me*, my wife responded, *I place great value upon discretion. It must be difficult, then, to have a famous husband at home*, Consuelo prodded further, and received a sharp response in return: *Is there anything more inglorious than fame?* Marta grabbed her glass and left the room. I remained in the room, continuing the interview, seething at my wife's snub. I thought for a second that it might, in fact, be jealousy, which would be something new coming from her; perhaps scorn, which really offended me. As we said goodbye, I apologized for Marta. Consuelo responded that, in Marta's place, she, too, would feel threatened. Then she shot me a different look, a smoldering look, which she hadn't dared to do before.

The bedroom was already dark, Marta was sleeping, or pretending to sleep, her back turned. I brushed my teeth and climbed into bed. I was angry. I dreamed of Consuelo, a warm, pleasant dream, which I told the editor about during our next and last official encounter. She acted surprised, she felt flattered, and took the chance to give me a long hug during our brief goodbye. We didn't speak for two weeks, there was no reason for it, our work was done; but the fantasy insisted on regaling me with nightly visits, recurring visions, and became increasingly real. In one, I sat before her, nude, as she took notes about my dick. Hence the shiver that climbed my neck when I received a handwritten note from Consuelo, delivered by the soap's PR lady. She suggested lunch, on the pretext of choosing photos. I scheduled for the following day, I had to see her, I was obsessed. I had never wanted to cheat on Marta, and it wasn't easy to admit that this was what I was about to do, or was already doing, at least in my imagination. Consuelo laid out a sheet of proofs, a series of negatives, a few of them circled with a Pilot pen. Me laughing, me serious, me at Marta's side. Marta. With the help of a magnifying glass, I noticed for the first time her gloomy expression in the photo. I saw myself married, a couple. *Is this really what I want?* I wondered, recalling my discomfort that afternoon when she locked herself in the bedroom without saying goodbye to the reporter. I chose the best poses, then faced the temptation before me. *So, Mario . . . ?* Consuelo said, as though that "so" contained a world of possibilities. You only live once. I paid the bill and took Ms. Trouble to my MP Lafer, bringing our professional relationship to a close. I drove with my hand on her thigh, as I'd done one day with Marta, toward Recreio. Back at her place, we devoured each other in the living room. There was no conversation, poetry, prose, nothing. I got dressed as soon as it was over and left. Consuelo wasn't one for talking either. She'd fallen for me. Back on the street, a bad feeling set in, in every way, reality didn't add up to expectation. I never called her again. I buried the editor in the back of the closet, along with twenty copies of the magazine. I didn't dare show it to Marta. Our sad photo on page four and the name Consuelo

Fontes there in the byline, just below the compromising title: "Passion." The only thing left of my lust was an awkward feeling. Consuelo's shrewd demeanor was no more than a facade, what was found inside was no different from the girls at the shoe store. But it was with her that I opened the portal, that I crossed the Rubicon of extramarital affairs. It was to her that I first told the story of my odyssey and I began to repeat it, to anyone who wished to listen or publish it. What before was an idea of the Mario I always wanted to be became the complete Mario, all I was. I cycled between soaps, plays, and films until I was graced with the role of the villain Augusto Reis, the man shot into space like a ball of fire after stealing from his business partners. Ninety percent of the viewership. Goodbye, sanity! I no longer fit within my own skin. Mother, friend, relative, or spouse, none of that existed anymore; not even the loss of my father could move me.

I LEARNED of his death between the first and second Sunday shows at a theater in Recife. The curtain went up three times that day. Three. Twenty-five hundred paying customers. Argan, the hypochondriac. Blessed Molière. The popularity of television in service of more and more paying customers. It had been six months of alternating between recording the soap and the nationwide tour, the phenomenon repeating itself in each city. I took the gangway to the dressing room; we had forty minutes until the next performance began. The set would continue on to Fortaleza while I spent the week in Porto de Galinhas, basking in the accolades in the arms of the actress who played my daughter. Our affair was well-known, I no longer bothered hiding it. Neither did Marta. I suspected that her admiration for a recently arrived exile from Europe, a former guerrilla fighter with political designs, had blossomed into a romance. Jealousy aside, I considered the tryst fair. Our long periods apart spared us from the arguments. We spoke by telephone as though nothing had changed. We avoided honest appraisals, maintaining relationships on the side without compromising our union.

I was retouching my makeup when the stage director walked in to tell me my wife was on the line, she'd called the theater.

That's strange, I thought. *Something wrong?* He wasn't sure how to respond. I crossed the backstage area with a bad feeling, passing through the labyrinth of doors that led to the administrative offices, made sure I was alone, and picked up. After a brief hesitation, Marta decided to be direct. *It's your father, Mario. My father? Yes*, she said. *Is he all right?* Pause. *No, Jorge had a stroke this afternoon, your mother ran to the hospital but he didn't make it.* He didn't make it. . . . Why avoid the term? *Death isn't a dirty word*, I reflected, irritated. *He's dead, is that it?* I roared back at her, as though her gentle demeanor were the real problem. *Yes, that's it*, Marta confirmed, *I feel awful. Feels . . . she feels.* I also tried to feel something but, to my shock, the only thing I felt was inconvenienced. Twenty-five hundred people there outside and Jorge decides to go and have a stroke. I wanted to go back to the stage, forget it all, postpone my mourning. The theater doesn't make exceptions for illness. *Don't go getting sick on me all of a sudden, Jorge Cardoso, not now*, I ruminated, *not tonight. I can't skip the next show*, I told Marta. She promised she'd look after Maria Amélia, take care of the paperwork, dutifully fulfill the role of daughter-in-law. She'd scheduled the burial for the next afternoon, I'd grab the nine o'clock flight and make it in time for the wake. The wake, one more thing to worry about, none of this was making sense. I feigned consternation, I tried every trick I knew, but the only thing I felt was the unsavory feeling of being forced to deal with a death. I didn't say anything to my colleagues. I told the young actress I had urgent business, putting off the beach. I strode onstage a man possessed, I battled for every joke, I won over the audience, as though acting were an antidote for mortality. I sauntered around, I made it happen, I proved myself greater than the pain, greater than death. Jorge wasn't going to take that from me.

"In the devil's name! If I were a doctor, I'd let him have it for his impudence. If he were ill, I'd let him die without help!"

There were five, count 'em, five curtain calls. Not content to merely applaud, the audience stomped on the ground, the theater roaring like a lion. It was a shame my father hadn't died on Saturday. Then I could have used my sacred commitment to the stage as an excuse and been free of the burial rites. But no, no one knows the hour.

The flight delayed due to a stop in Belém, I landed just in time to carry the casket. Marcelo, my ripped cousin, took the opposite handle, Gomes the third, we were at the peak of our partnership. Carine and my Aunt Neusa trailed behind, supporting my inconsolable grandmother. The first signs of her illness would appear a few months after the loss of her son, perhaps because of it. My mother soldiered on, her hand on the casket. She said nothing. She had left her tears in the bedroom after an entire night without sleep; now she would serenely assume her role as widow. Photographers were waiting for us at the exit to the cemetery, I was happy to see them there. I played the orphan and struck a tired pose. Vanity, it was all vanity. I'd loved my father; at some point, who knows, I would mourn his loss.

We brought Maria Amélia to sleep at our house. She asked for a sleeping pill and fell into a deep sleep. Marta and I went to the living room. It was harder to lie to my wife; my bitterness was obvious. *Do you want to talk?* she ventured to make first contact. *I don't want anything*, I answered sharply. Marta wanted to know if she'd done something wrong. *I don't know, did you?* I opened the duel, for the pure pleasure of trampling all over her. I didn't give a damn about her affair with the leftist idol, but I did my best to leave her feeling guilty, a screw had come loose in me.

For the last year we'd been facing a serious marital crisis. Marta became pregnant and I refused to recognize the child as my own. Worse, I asked her to get rid of it. *We have time*, I said, *why do this now?* I'd tried to kiss her, but she'd recoiled. I realized the hurt I'd caused her, but I stood firm. I told her that I loved her, that I wanted to carry on as we always had, lovers, free. Marta pretended to understand, but she never forgave me. The next morning, without my knowing it, she checked into a clinic and only returned home at the end of the day. She came back clammed up. I regretted my lack of tact, but I only understood what an insult it had been when I saw her walk in the door without a word, changed. Her upbringing kept her from outbursts. We barely exchanged a word for more than a month. I kept on playing the romantic, I flattered her at every opportunity, but my refusal to become a father had cut our future in half. Between love and self-love, I always chose the latter. That was the measure of my smallness as a man and as an actor. Marta was just part of the scenery, I didn't want her for anything beyond myself.

We would laugh in public, but we maintained our distance between our four walls. We were never intimate again. The exiled hero showed up months after the incident, but it was his fruit, I'm certain. The two met at the university, at a talk for sociology students. They became friends. The ex-guerrilla, who'd broken with the left, was concerned with subjects that still didn't exist in a Brazil that had just emerged from dictatorship. Feminism, environmentalism, sexual liberation. A vegetarian, even his farts smelled sweet, as they say. The newcomer attracted a legion of followers. Marta's refinement, her intelligence, everything about her, awoke the reborn martyr's interest, they became fast friends, and she ended up getting involved in his campaign for public office. They saw each other more than we saw each other. We dined together a few times, with me playing the part of the liberal as I gnawed at a prime cut of steak just to offend the sanctimonious martyr. I was afraid of losing her, I didn't want that. I knew I deserved her indifference, her distance, my horns, to put it bluntly. No one just forgets an abortion. I sought distance, I resolved my jealousy with honest partners and cured myself with Argan in the limelight. It was love, what she was feeling, and not for me. *Leave it alone, one day it'll be over*, I thought, *one day she'll come back*.

Back from the funeral, I took my uneasiness out on Marta. *Did I do something to you, Mario? I don't know, did you?* I responded. She got the message and grabbed her purse. Marta never responded to provocation. *You going to meet the politician?* I jeered. *No*, she said, *I'm going to watch the sun go down on the beach*. And off she went. Only then did I cry, for me, for us, and for my father.

I WOULD CRY other times, fresh cries, worse ones, until I learned to no longer cry at all. Failure instructs and strengthens. *Don't think, Mario, just do*, that was the mantra I repeated to myself, that morning in front of the mirror before I stepped up to the gallows.

I had breakfast with Maria Amélia and Carine. I browsed the newspaper. The two of them had woken up early, they had plans to go out that afternoon. They laughed among themselves, like schoolgirls trading secrets. During the previous months, they'd taken to going everywhere together, they spent the day out and only came back in the evening. They had been playing. The casino. So great was my grief that I'd overlooked the credit card bills and long hours out. I had suspected they'd been gambling the day that Carine, seeing my coming into the office, hurried to shut her laptop. Thanks to the amenities there at home, she'd joined Facebook. Glancing over her shoulder, I'd managed to read an ad offering free transportation to elderly women who wanted to risk their savings via illegal gambling. My cousin's ears perked up, I almost unleashed everything on her but held back, I preferred to forgive her. My mother was another person, she woke up happy, did her makeup, went out;

later, she returned on a high, beaming. *Let her have her game*, I thought, *what harm is there in her addiction?* I asked Carine to not place any wild bets and to see after Maria Amélia. It was better than seeing her sitting around worried, sleeping on the couch, suffering on account of an abortion that had never taken place or the illusion of a one-way marriage with her son.

We ate as though life were under control. I asked about their plans and, trading complicit glances, they told me they were going to have lunch out and then catch a movie. I pretended to believe them. Neither one was interested in what I was going to do in São Paulo, and I also didn't care to share. We kissed goodbye as though we were the Holy Family and I left that bright Guanabara Bay morning behind to face a rainy Saturday in São Paulo. The heavy sky was a more faithful translation of my state of being.

†

I headed for the studio in a remote neighborhood. I was welcomed effusively by the production crew. Water, coffee, a private dressing room, new towels. Gomes called to know whether I'd arrived all right; Milena appeared with a smile on her face, bringing the client with her to give me a welcoming. I was kind, I posed for photos and pretended to be happy. Everyone cleared out. I put on my robe and was led to the makeup room. I relaxed in the barber's chair, the makeup artist massaged my face and I enjoyed the peace of her delicate fingers. Foundation, shadow, blush. She asked me to have a look, she wanted to know if I was happy.

I had a look. The ghost in the mirror, the dark Max Factor circles. The fake beard applied with gloss. The lines of my face drawn out in pencil. The old man. *Ready?* the assistant asked. *Always*, came my solemn response.

I went back to the dressing room to put on the rags that would make the figure complete. The attendant adjusted the ragged cloak, the crown weighed down on me as though made of thorns. Lear, my foe. Slowly, I walked down the long hallway that led to the studio.

Bright lights, heat like a stove, the desert. The director approached me, eager to help, and explained the scene. The monarch would stumble to the throne and then sit, exhausted. *Our poorest beggars are in the poorest thing superfluous*, the voice-over would say offstage. Relieved, I would unroll a thin layer of toilet paper and, speaking straight into the camera, would recite a line from Act 2, Scene 4 of the play.

"Allow not nature more than nature needs, Man's life's as cheap as beast's."

A wide shot, of me seated on a glimmering latrine, the tiny roll in hand, was to merge with the image of the product, white, immaculate as the Holy Virgin. *Noble: for those who never lose their dignity*, would come the closing title card. The client started in over the *lack of class* in the voice-over. *It's offensive to the poor*, he argued, worried about displeasing the rising working class. *It's Shakespeare!* the ad man huffed, as though his creation had any relationship to the Bard. We lost nearly an hour to the tiresome argument, until the client was convinced that they would resolve the issue later, in postproduction. The cocky little ad man stopped his strutting and the director gave the order for the train to roll. I gave a resigned sigh, it was almost over, almost. Despite my dishonor, I would leave there with my comedy of errors remedied. They checked the focus, we rehearsed for the cameras, I dragged myself through the sand on the floor until I found myself before the bright, polished throne. As I performed my task, I went over in my mind the series of events that had landed me there. The success I had known as an actor, the detours, and a forty-year career all down the toilet. The end of the line, death, who knows, even the resurrection. They demanded a smile during the close-up, with the toilet paper in hand. I smiled, I didn't have a choice. I went through with the whole ordeal. I took off the beard, removed the dark circles, but the wrinkles remained intact. I had aged, a lot, that afternoon. I didn't say goodbye to the team, I didn't say a word to anyone, I left the tomb through the back door. The rain had passed and the sun colored the sky an illusive orange, completing one more day of its journey across Earth. I sucked down a cigarette until the filter grew hot. How many of those had I smoked since the very first, decades earlier, during a meeting of the top brass of a multinational tobacco company?

†

At the top of a building in São Paulo, I sat at the table, surrounded by forty senior executives, waiting to be introduced as the new face of the brand. When asked, I responded that no, I didn't smoke, I'd never smoked. An awkward silence followed at the oval table. The director of the agency pulled a pack from his pocket and offered me one. *It's never too late to begin*, he said. I grabbed the cylinder and a tall American man, so blond he was nearly albino, held out a lighter; I leaned forward with the cigarette, inhaled without coughing, and debonairly exhaled. An ovation. Everyone repeated the gesture and together we all smoked ourselves silly in diabolical fraternity. How many people had died and become addicted because of that commercial? Too many to count, I suppose, me included, but I had never been ashamed of doing it, unlike now.

I tossed the butt on the ground and extinguished it with my foot. I hoped my bad habit would shorten my life. It would be a relief, I thought, to disappear, to vanish from here. My ambition had morphed into *a walking shadow, a poor player, that struts and frets his hour* before a roll of toilet paper. I took the plane back to Rio. My Rio, as bankrupt as I was. I didn't say a word in the empty plane, chewing my stale peanuts and drinking a flat Coca-Cola. I opened the door of my house dragging my shoes. Maria Amélia and Carine were still out roaming the streets. I cleansed my soul in the shower, had dinner in the empty room, and snored in front of the TV.

†

I recorded Lot's final breaths in a papier-maché cave located in a studio with no AC. I sweated like a hog in the sealed-off hole, but the role didn't demand much. I didn't have to yell, run, or even memorize my lines. In the original, the villain's daughters get him drunk and procreate with him in a mission to fulfill the command to be fruitful and multiply. Holiness aside, incest was unthinkable during prime time. The writer resolved this canonical shamelessness with me getting drunk and having a dialogue with the unmarried spawn opening up about their fear of becoming old maids. A word to the wise is more than enough.

The final chapter of *Sodom* aired fifteen days later. My mother watched with great interest, from her sofa, seated next to Carine, asking me why I looked so worn out. *It's the Bible, Maria Amélia, it's the Bible*, I responded. Commercial break: Noble, the toilet paper. My mother didn't recognize me and got up to fetch a glass of water. Carine's eyes grew wide, she asked me whether that was really me. *It is, Carine, it is*, I confirmed. She started to chuckle, a derisive smirk. Maria Amélia called out, Carine got up to help, and I began scanning through the channels. The damn thing was being shown on a massive scale, cable and broadcast. I ran to my Web browser. Five-second callouts leapt across the screen. *One . . . two . . . three . . . four. . . .* I wanted to see the camera cut. There was the latrine, the five seconds lasted until I sat on the latrine . . . this was the hook to convince users not to skip the ad.

I considered becoming a shut-in.

Just then, I remembered an actress who lived to regret posing nude for a men's magazine. Soraia Ribeiro was her name. I saw Soraia in the street, at a time when I still walked around like a hero; we hadn't come across one another since the last soap. I told her I'd seen her, I couldn't remember where, when I realized that it had been in the infamous magazine. A cameraman, wearing a sickening smile, had dragged me to the corner of the studio and opened up the main spread. *Did you catch Soraia, Mario? What an ass!* he said. I had forgotten all about it until I noticed the actress's crestfallen expression there on the sidewalk. Soraia's splayed body flashed across my mind for a second, she took note, and wished me a gloomy goodbye. She was full of regret, no sum was great enough to compensate for her exposure. Now it was my turn.

I unplugged the computer, the television, I avoided newspapers, magazines, and the radio. A year, my god, a year of Soraia ahead of me. I took an antidepressant, administered by the psychiatrist who treated Maria Amélia. With the Lot routine concluded, I was waiting to go back to the daily grind a few months later, in the sequel to the religious soap, where I was to take on the role of Laban. On my doctor's advice, I began taking walks along the beach, in an attempt to occupy my downtime and remember that there was still some beauty in life.

†

One sunny afternoon, I was walking calmly, admiring the day, my humors subdued by the advances in psychiatry. All was well until I found myself before a bus with Lear clasping a roll of Noble emblazoned on its rear. I tried to divert my attention but the stoplight turned red, fixing the image before me. Distracted, I didn't see the gang of pint-size thieves close in around me. One of them, a devilish little bastard missing one of his front teeth, looked at the ad and then brashly turned to address me. *I saw you on television*, he said, then asked for some money. I said no. *Come on, uncle*, he insisted. I turned my back and walked away. As revenge, the little twerp made a fart sound with his tongue between his lips and invited his friends to join in his jeers. The spark plug got the rest of the little demons all fired up, and they began imitating their leader, forming a buffoon's quintet. I picked up the pace, but the gang was coming fast. Three of them were banging out fart sounds with their mouths, another chimed in with the bass, the youngest marked the beat, his right hand in his armpit, flapping his wings to produce the sound effect. They started singing funk. *King of the can, crown on his head, king of the can, crapping in his hand.* . . . I sped around in a rage, which only made it worse. The youngest dropped his pants and showed me his rear. I got into the first taxi and left the orchestra behind me; but the jingle played on loop until the car had pulled away.

I asked if I could smoke, the driver said OK. The radio was playing some second-rate hit, an American singer meowing like a cat in heat. The driver asked where I was going. Where? Straight to the grave. I gave him my home address, I wasn't ever leaving again. I gazed at the beach, the majestic sea against the autumn sky. The regal indifference of the postcards. Arriving home, I couldn't wait to pull down the shades, I locked myself in the bedroom, swallowed a handful of sleeping pills, and went lights out to forget it all. Not a single dream, memory, or image to pursue me. A pharmaceutical blessing. I was torn out of my trance by the relentless ring of the telephone on the bedside table. My hand sought the button, I picked up.

On the other end of the line a distressed Carine, she wanted to know if my mother had come home. It took me a few minutes to collect my thoughts. What did she mean, come home, hadn't they left together? I looked in the bedrooms, the kitchen, and the living room, not a trace of Maria Amélia. My cousin broke down, weeping hysterically. A police sting had burst in on the illicit gambling venue on Rua Pompeu Loureiro, where she and my mother had gone that afternoon. As they always did, the law enforcement officers let the elderly habitués go and detained the rest, my cousin among them. Despite her appeals, Maria Amélia had been sent outside. She had seemed confused. Carine was calling from a jail in Copacabana, she wasn't going to be booked or let go anytime soon. Her fear that my mother didn't remember the way home was suddenly justified. *Hurry, Mario, hurry*, she urged, *she can't have gone far!*

AUNT NEUSA hugged me as though I were her own son. *You can always count on me, Mario, on Marcelo; Carine, as you know, liked Amélia a great deal.* Thanks to Tijuca, my mother had the honor of a funeral Mass. I, who am not a believer, was thankful for the show of support. That's what religions are for. The casket had just rolled down the crematorium assembly line. How stupid of me to refuse to become a father. Maybe I'd be a grandfather today and have someone to provide me consolation. That's what families are for. *Take me with you, Aunt Neusa,* I begged, *I can't go home alone.*

Crossing through the tunnel, I was filled with remorse for having lost time between morgues and hospitals. I should have guessed that Maria Amélia would head straight for the beach and throw herself into the sea. Even the location was the same. I should have run to the beach, near Rua Miguel Lemos, where the ocean currents form a deceptive graveyard. Too late. Aunt Neusa could see I was restless, took my hand in hers, and repeated that she was there to help.

I climbed the steps that wound through the three-floor building, the crooked steps, a tough climb even for adult legs. The giant rats from the putrid little stream of water, the melted butter on the kitchen table. My grandmother in the shadows of the old home office. Aunt Neusa made a point of laying out a lace tablecloth. We sat down, just like when we were kids, Marcelo chewing his food with his mouth wide open. What before had triggered nausea now kept the sadness away. His tongue, turning his food over between his teeth, something recognizable, familiar. Carine ate in silence, she was feeling remorse, too, for having taken Maria Amélia gambling, for not having kept the police from sending her outside. *It's God who chooses the hour*, Aunt Neusa proffered wisely when she noticed her daughter's guilt. We agreed, even without giving the maxim much credence. *It happened the way it had to*, she concluded. *Can you see your grandmother?* We returned to the dark crack in the doorway where the family elder wandered between two worlds. *God, what a satirist*, I thought. *A son of a bitch who strikes my father dead at the height of my happiness and takes Maria Amélia when I still needed her*. If the wretch had any sense of justice, he would have snatched my grandmother from that bedroom years ago instead of leaving her to wither away.

We watched the news on the plastic-covered couch. Carine served milk pudding. In the break between one bad story and another, the Noble commercial burst across the screen. My aunt, containing a smile, cried out, "Oh, Mario, I can't stand watching you do this!" Her grandson, Matias, looked at the screen, then to me, and burst into a laughter. The boy's no-qualms attitude was contagious and I gave in. *It's ridiculous, I know*, I said, surprised at my sudden good humor. The conversation turned to my acting career. Everyone said what huge fans they were of the religious soap, singling out the meteor crash for particular praise. *It was very well done*, Marcelo exclaimed, as though he were capable of telling his ass from his elbow, and it felt good to still be part of the imagination of old Tijuca. Aunt Neusa told me to make myself at home, offered to sleep in the living room and for me to stay in the bedroom. I refused, thanked her for everything, and kissed her hands.

Carine would collect her junk from my apartment, she was moving back to the ancestral slum, I would find a place for my mother's belongings and face the emptiness. We agreed to talk later that week, to take care of details. I left late, grabbed a taxi in an abandoned Praça Sáenz Peña, there was no game today, and I crossed the tunnel in silence. I had never imagined I would miss my mother so much.

I sat on the armchair with the lights out and for a long time I didn't move. That was when a bottle of whiskey looked at me suggestively from the shelf. *Maybe it will help*, I thought. I did what I should not have done: I drank. I drank too much. The lack of prospects, the aspirations of an actor reduced to a series of biblical roles on a religious TV channel, the lack of love, of a wife, of a mother and a father, the end of the line, I drowned in the bottle.

I repeated the routine the next day, and the next, and the following day, and the day after that.

The weeks passed in the drunkenness of the first swig, without anyone noticing or demanding that I stop. My beard grew long, my hair too, showers became infrequent. I told the cleaning lady to come only once a week, I didn't want any witnesses. I wandered naked around the apartment, I watched cartoons, cracked up at Woody the Woodpecker, and collapsed in whatever spot my legs managed to take me. I thought it was part of the mourning process, that it would all pass, but no.

†

It was three months after Maria Amélia's death that my cousin finally showed her face. She had called to schedule a visit, but I hadn't registered any more than that. Still with her own set of keys, she opened the door without knocking, called out but received no response. I remember hearing a scream and then plunging back into my habitual lethargy. She'd freaked out. When she found me naked, sprawled out in the hallway, she thought I was dead and, alarmed, phoned her mother. They stuck me in a cold bath over my protests. Carine stood vigil while her mother cleaned bits of leftover food from furniture, separated the dirty clothes in the laundry room sink, threw the rotten food out the fridge, made the bed, and cleaned the apartment. If she had two brain cells, perhaps she could replace Maria Amélia. No. I wouldn't be able to handle living with her. Aunt Neusa prepared some chicken soup, I lifted the spoon to my mouth like a lost little boy, and I patiently listened to her motivational speech. *A young man, famous* . . . the awful cliché. I pretended I was listening, counting the minutes until I was free of them. Aunt Neusa left, threatening to come back later and put her daughter in charge of daily check-ins to ensure I was all right. I played the sweet nephew, put the two of them in the elevator, and struggled back to the door. The night before, I'd twisted my ankle without noticing it, and now it was swollen. I limped about and, professional deformities and all, I did a half-assed Long John Silver, singing the refrain about a bottle of rum. *More like Peg-Leg*, I thought, the villain of *Pluft, the Little Ghost*, another hard drinker with no scruples. There would always be a role for me, even if it was in plays for children. My good mood went down the drain as soon as I noticed that Aunt Neusa had poured out all the whiskey and left the empty bottles, proof of her crime, lined up in the service hallway. I nearly kicked them all, then grabbed my wallet and went out.

Not content with a binge at the corner bar, I decided to stretch my legs. A woman with two missing teeth reminded me of the Lapa hookers, the ones who had taught Raquel to be Neusa Sueli, the joining of flesh that buried my Helena. I shed tears of longing for the Russian woman as I recited the plot of Uncle Vanya to the drunk lady at the bar.

Lapa! I told the taxi driver. I wanted to see if the musty old bordello was still there. I would grab any old Neusa, go into the VIP room, and throw myself from the window. I would meet Raquel again on the other side. Brilliant plan. The driver asked for more specifics, and I went nuts. *Lapa is Lapa, for chrissake*, I answered rudely, *it's on the second floor, it's a mansion with stairs!* The man kept driving without argument. On his fifth attempt to rid himself of his blitzed passenger, he dropped me at a secluded whorehouse halfway up the hill to Santa Teresa. I wanted him to travel back in time, I insisted on returning to the old brothel or to the room at the cheap motel where Raquel had sucked the bastard's cock. I wanted to beat the hell out of that greaser, take her home and look after her for the rest of our lives. *It was Neusa who killed Raquel*, I reasoned aloud. The taxi driver kept a wary eye on me. *All these roles are crap!* I bellowed like a tenor. *These writers . . . are a bunch of nutcases!* I grabbed hold of the wheel, convinced I would find the spot myself. The guy had had enough. He drove to the top of the hill and braked, threatening to take me to the police station if I refused to leave his cab. *Idiot*, I stammered under my breath as I tossed a fifty into the back the seat. I slammed the door, tripped over myself, and fell. The car sped off, rubber screeching. Everything smelled like shit. I walked into the place, ordered a double shot and demanded to speak to the manager. A woman with awful makeup appeared, escorted by some muscle, I could sense authority in her. *I want to speak with Raquel*, I said. *Tell her to come down, say that Mario's here. Cardoso, Mario Cardoso, the actor, a friend of hers*. The madame claimed she knew no Raquel but offered a range of Shirleys to resolve my problem. Four of them came in a group, cell phones in the air, shooting selfies. I lost my patience. I pushed the bodyguard onto the leeches and tore through the hallway door, screaming the name of the dead woman. I walked in on people on all fours, on their backs, on their bellies. A wild rumpus with no rhyme or reason. I found myself in the same gutter where I'd been dropped fifteen minutes earlier.

I listened to the sounds of the city, the night birds, the barking of dogs, the random car climbing the filthy, narrow street. *There's still one left*, I thought. *Gomes*. The eternal Gomes, the fraternal Gomes, Gomes the counselor. All I needed was to go and see him. We would plan out the future together, we would take the toilet paper commercial out of circulation, I would turn my back on religious dramas and return to the scene with *Macbeth*. *Macbeth*, not *Lear*. This time, no Steins, no scenery, or rotisserie chickens. No sponsor. God and I and the stage.

Before daybreak, I rang the doorbell at the gate to the building on Rua General Glicério, where Gomes had lived since we'd met. I was in high spirits, the doorman was fast asleep. I clapped my hands, scraped the key against the gate until he woke up, I shouted into the intercom. *Mario Cardoso! Gomes is expecting me!* The guy rang the apartment, pissed, I could see his expression through the glass.

Gomes greeted me, sleepy or apprehensive, I couldn't tell, his pajamas and cheeks wrinkled. He asked whether something had happened. *Do you have any whiskey?* I asked. He didn't drink, I settled for a glass of water. I downed the glass in one gulp, complained about the dark room, turned on a lamp without asking, and launched into my speech.

I babbled nonstop, on my feet, weaving between the furniture. There wasn't a clear surface in the entire place, a sort of sober-kitsch of the 1980s. Gomes stood at the door, aghast. I was going to say to hell with Noble, the religious network, I would start rehearsals for *Macbeth* that same week, no directors, I had enough experience; I would find a theater in São

Paulo, I'd rent a small apartment there. Three, four months of preparation, it didn't matter, it would premiere when it was ready. Gomes was mute. I finished my rant. *Are you sure you don't have some whiskey?* I asked, it had been more than an hour since my last drink. *Mario . . .* he stammered, looking to the floor, had he not heard what I said? Seeing I was about go off, Gomes measured his words. He advised me to rest, we would discuss it all the next day, when I'd had a chance to sober up. There's nothing that angers a drunk more than the accusation he's had too much to drink. *I am sober!* I asserted, repeating the part about the end of my career in toilet paper, my farewell to the Bible, and a one-man *Macbeth. Of course, Mario, tomorrow, at my office. . . . To hell with the office, Gomes!* I sat at the table to do the math: costumes, lighting, good lighting, there was a new kid, in Curitiba, how much did a flight come to? *Mario . . .* he repeated. I looked at Gomes, his exhaustion, his silence. The alcoholic roller-coaster was beginning its descent. I begged him to listen. Gomes sat down patiently, held my hand like a father, said that he understood my pain, the death of Maria Amélia, my professional crisis. *There's always a spring to be found when you hit rock-bottom*, he reminded me, and offered a place to crash. *Sleep? Who wanted to sleep? I do, Mario*, he said, *it's four-twenty in the morning.* Gomes's lack of initiative, his reluctance to discuss the plan for my salvation, the stuffy environment; I wasn't going to stop, not now that I'd found a way out. I jumped to my feet, the chair fell back, he sought to bring me to my senses, repeating *Mario . . . Mario, what? Mario who?* I said and pushed him away. Gomes tried to lead me to the guest room. I walked backward, he toward me, his arms surrounding me like an octopus. *I don't need you for a fucking thing*, I yelled. Then I threatened to leave him, leave the office, I blamed him for having introduced me to Mota, for hiding that dandy's tricks, selling my image to a line of goddamn toilet paper. I told him about the little pricks on the beach, the humiliation caused by that vulgar advertisement. I threatened him, saying I'd bring all that shit out into public, but the response was always the same: *Mario . . . Mario . . . Mario. . . .* Possessed, I raised my fist into the air, Gomes's jaw dropped, and so as not to drive my hand through his face, I grabbed a Chinese porcelain lion from the shelf and shattered it across the floor. The accountant told me to leave, threatened to call the police. I laughed, saying I'd go, but not without having my whiskey. *Where do you hide the bottle?* I ran around opening the cupboards, tossing everything out. Gomes lost his patience and grappled with me. Round and round we went, he pushing me to the door, I providing counterweight in the direction of the window. I clutched the curtain, he tried a poorly placed uppercut, the rod couldn't hold, the cloth came down like a cascade, we lost our balance, horns locked, I steadied myself against the window, but Gomes, big ol' Gomes, slipped on the chenille, and was launched into space. His feet, one at a time, rose in a somersault. His arm loosened from around my neck, I looked to the side in time to witness the gravitational miracle. Striped pajamas cutting an arc through the air, his heft crashing over the windowsill, his backside headed for the abyss. I tried to grab him by the pant leg, by his slippers, but there was no force great enough to prevent his collapse. I heard him howl, a long lament as he slipped from me, followed by a cracking sound as he hit the ground.

A dog barked, a car alarm sounded, that was it.

†

It was good, to die and to kill. To be hit in the back by a blank, to arch one's back, simulating the impact; to burst the bag of blood between one's teeth, allow the red liquid to flow from the mouth, to stumble and then fall, take one last breath. To keep one's eyes open in the stupor of that final moment. Renato Brandão threw himself from the London Bridge, as the aging leading lady looked on, in the disastrous prime-time remake of *Vertigo*. It was good. Very good. But nothing could rival the thrill of grabbing the revolver and pulling the trigger. Bang! Bang! Bang! End of episode. Augusto Reis, the archvillain, shot up five in the soap *The Rescue*. The slave driver José Dias tied the young mestiza girl to the tree and beat her until she bled. It was good, to exercise cruelty, to be vile, a killer, to kill, to die and then come back to life. But there was no joy at that moment or at any time thereafter. I didn't move, my fingers clinging to the window, waiting for Gomes to call to me from below, for the director to bellow *Cut*, for someone to compliment me for the scene, as someone invariably did. No.

Reluctantly, I stretched my neck outside and looked around.

Gomes was sprawled out, his legs crooked. The blood pooling around his inert body. The deserted garage of that old building in Laranjeiras.

PART II

Imagination dead imagine.

BECKETT,
ALL STRANGE AWAY

FOR MONTHS, Mario felt his absence. The emptiness that seized him at the window. At that moment, he'd remained where he was, his stiff fingers clutching the glass, it wasn't long before the cops showed up. He quietly climbed into the paddy wagon and was taken to the station. He didn't understand what the lawyer had told him, nor did he react to his sentence. The doorman could attest to his drinking binge and the neighbors had heard the scuffle. The judge concluded that Gomes had been pushed. Fifteen years. Mario listened silently to the prison director's lecture without making out his words and walked like a robot through the long gallery of the jail. He crossed between the concrete dividers of the immense cell, and settled into a raw foam mattress on the floor, wedged between two bunk beds. There wasn't enough room for everyone. A line of a hundred convicts waited in the barracks, their hands behind their backs and eyes low. As he crossed the corridor of dark faces, Mario kept his attention to the floor, forgetting to look around him. The stench didn't faze him. He wasn't there. He was somewhere between two different worlds, like his grandmother in Tijuca. He didn't suffer, he wasn't present. His mind, lost in the succession of events, had abandoned logic.

Aware of the inmate's fragility, the director bunked him in cell D-7 of the evangelical ward, the cleanest. God helps those in need. The outside wall, unlike the filthy plaster in the first half of the cell-block, was decorated with biblical passages. Simple paintings in naive colors, in the style of ads for small-town barber shops. They portrayed scenes from the Old and New Testaments: the Sermon on the Mount, Christ on the cross, and the Last Supper; Moses and the Red Sea, Daniel in the den of lions. But it was the last picture, right next to the iron bars of D-7, that caught Mario's eye. Sodom was engulfed in flames, after the impact of the meteor. Sodom. The scene that, millennia ago, a vague memory, he had recorded in a field in Jacarepaguá. In the foreground, Lot, his daughters, and the statue of the mother-wife turned to salt. Lot. Mario recognized his features. They were his own. That was him. Turbaned and bearded. The prisoners, faithful viewers of the religious channel, had followed *Sodom* on two small televisions, one above the cell door, the other above the hole that led to the bathroom, at the far end of the dungeon.

Since he didn't open his mouth, Mario was baptized Lot. So they called him. Lot woke up, went to bed; Lot was docile and reserved. He didn't play ball, he didn't read, he didn't pray. He barely ate and curled up in a corner when the prisoners were led out to take some sun. Mario, meanwhile, he engaged in confusing dialogues, quarrels and arguments, intense soliloquies all between the walls of his skull. Mario was Lear, Vado, and Renato Brandão. Argan and José Dias. Augusto Reis, Vicente, and Riobaldo. He rode across the wide-open fields, cursed the

slut and threw himself from London Bridge, where one day he'd
worked. What came when, the actual order of events, remained
a mystery to him. Nothing ahead of him, only the disorder of
what he'd left behind. Powerful waves, crashing against the
bones of his skull, an endless headache. At times, he remembered his father, or thought he had a sister. He remembered
his mother, on a beach, but was slow to remember why.

Aunt Neusa dragged Carine to visit him. The daughter
hated these outings. She panicked in the fenced-in quad wedged
between the favela of Mangueira and the zoo of the Quinta da
Boa Vista, where Mario lived, or very nearly. His aunt would
hand him the soap for scabies, some Tylenol, and sleeping pills.
Lacking the resources to treat the prisoners, the government
had allowed family members to provide medication. In addition
to the medicine, Neusa also brought her nephew crackers and
cigarettes. Mario had forgotten everything except nicotine.
On Sundays, after they'd left the prison, his aunt wept in the
subway car. Before returning home, she stopped to pray for her
nephew at a nearby church. She took the fan from the bedroom
and gave it to him when his first summer there rolled around.
Mario greeted her lukewarmly, showing no anger but also no
tenderness. *I think he's gone crazy*, Neusa would say to her son,
Marcelo, but she never abandoned her visits. *It's for Jorge and
Amélia*, she would say, *I take care of Mario for them.*

Jackson followed his friend's drama via the newspapers and
also visited. The first time, he took a pack of lighters, which was
confiscated at the door. It was never returned to him. *Mario,
you son of a bitch*, he said, when he saw the ghost, *what sort of*

shit did you get yourself mixed up in? But Mario didn't respond. He stared into space and bear-hugged his friend each time they said goodbye.

Greta Garbo took a fancy to the actor. She was his fan, even before she met him. She resolved to adopt him. She was the only one who called him Mario; *Mario Cardoso*, he insisted with the others, *the actor!* Greta was transferred to the evangelical wing after a misunderstanding in C-4. Under threat, she pretended to convert but was forced to give up her nom de guerre. She couldn't stand Anderson, her baptismal name, and that was why she fought for Lot's Mario. With the Pastor's permission, Greta dragged her idol's mattress to the foot of hers and lied down right there, like a trained dog. The Pastor was the authority in D-7, he kept God's peace in the precinct. A clever man, he quickly realized the advantage of assuming the role of religious leader. His mother had taught him how to pray, he'd studied up to high school and read the Bible with great ability. The evangelical sector smelled better and was safe. The Pastor had enemies. At dawn, he would read short verses out loud, from Matthew, Mark, John, and Luke; then, he saw to the scuffles. A former drug trafficking boss, he delivered one of the kingpins in the Jacaré favela to the police. He coveted the leadership for himself. Acting as a snitch for the cops, he had a death warrant out for him issued by the command of his own faction, he machine-gunned three in his escape and found himself with nowhere to go, in that prison without a commander, where the worst sort of scum lived piled one on top of the other. Rapists, killers, armed robbers, pedophiles, and drug traffickers counting the days until they reached parole. Some of them never left. Others left only to return soon after. Prison was a way of life for those forgotten convicts. Two thousand five hundred men, stacked on top of each other in a hangar built for just over a thousand, under the watch of six skinny guards. The gutter of gutters in a country with no sewage system.

Greta had stuck a knife in a client's chest. He was an army sergeant. He died in his sleep. *The jackass threatened me with a revolver*, she swore. She enjoyed recounting the story to an indifferent Mario while showing him a copy of her passport bearing stamps from all the countries of Europe she'd been to. Italy, France, Spain; Rome, Ibiza, and Marseilles. At times, she would apply lipstick on him when she thought he was too pale. Mario didn't care. He didn't mind being the former transvestite's pet.

†

And so six months of his hundred and eighty-month sentence passed, when suddenly Greta dragged him before the television. *The soap's about to begin*, she said cheerfully. He obeyed and got to his feet, looking at the screen, leaning against someone else's bed. He recognized Lineu, in the skin of the very same Abraham, climbing the mount hand in hand with a boy. *Take now your son, your only son, Isaac*, God's voice thundered, *and offer him as a sacrifice on a mountain I will tell you of*. Mario paid no attention to the Divine One, it was his colleague who aroused his interest. He pointed to the screen and walked forward, he wanted to see Lineu up close. Greta was shocked, it was the first time she'd seen him react to anything.

She ran forward to open up a path for him, kicking the others aside. Mario drew close to the image as though overcome with a vision. *But where is the lamb?* the miniature actor asked. His father did not respond. Mario gazed at Lineu with the knife raised above his head, his anguished and determined face. Deus reverberated off-screen, putting an end to the infanticide; Lineu wept and Mario applauded, in tears. Greta comforted him. Mario dreamed of Lineu that night. Wearing a diaper, Gloucester slept in the transvestite's bunk. Mario became a rabid viewer of the series he should have had a part in.

Abraham's death, in the thirtieth episode, marked an important change in Mario's disposition. As he watched Lineu close his eyes, he understood that he would never see him again. He became depressed. Lineu no more. He longed to see him. Then, with some difficulty, he expressed his desire to go to school, where they had paper and pen. He wanted to write a note. Greta took on the mission and asked one of the cleaners, an inmate with authorization to circulate throughout the prison, to send word to the volunteer teacher. Taken to the little room in the division between the cell-block and the administrative offices, Mario sat before the page, but all that came to him was confusion. He gave the blank page back to the teacher and returned to his cell. Even though he no longer cared, he continued watching the soap. On days they went outside, when the teacher was present, he would walk to the school and sit there staring at the page, unable to overcome his writer's block.

Mario began to recover his sanity in stages. Now, he would trade short bits of conversation with Greta and thank her each time she cleared his tray or defended him. One day, after once again failing to scribble on the page, he hazarded entering the library, located next to the school. The empty shelves held a few scarce volumes, most of them self-help or religious texts. There was no Machado, no Graciliano Ramos, and no Shakespeare; no Nelson Rodrigues, Drummond, or Amado, there was no one in that book desert. Mario missed books, something that he'd almost forgotten existed. At night, he began taking note of the others' movements. The Pastor, trailed by a group, dug out a cell phone they'd lodged in the wall and began making secret phone calls. One of them issued threats, another whispered, simulating a kidnapping. The Pastor negotiated the ransoms. They counted on the help of partners on the outside who collected the ransoms from the poor suckers and split them with those on the inside. It wasn't easy to come to terms with one's own misfortune. Fear was part of it. Mario felt uneasy in his white skin. He was in the minority there. A feeling he'd never had in the circles in which he moved when he was still Mario. Greta, white and feminine, was stronger than he was. He felt fragile, he tried to return to his former lethargy, but it was too late.

Each time he watched the fifty-episode religious soap, he emerged from the limbo that had engulfed him. Laban, future son to Jacob, Isaac's grown son, was introduced into the plot. That was the role Mario was to play, had he not run off the rails. Squished between his prison pals, he watched a mediocre actor, with the unfailing turban and the pointy beard, take his place.

A vulgar clone of the old Mario, the insolent man twisted his face into all sorts of configurations, while he sat there, in the sarcophagus. Jealousy, regret, perhaps even resentment, who knows? Mario turned around and lay back down in his ditch. It had been ages since he'd felt that sort of anger. It was good and bad. Lazarus resurrected by resentment. *Seven years Jacob served as a shepherd for Laban, lovely Rachel's father.* Camões. The verses his mother loved to recite aloud, for the simple pleasure of listening to the sonority of the words. Laban, Camões, Maria Amélia. He wanted his life back. He wept for his mother, understood the reason he'd associated her with the beach. He contemplated suicide, but he lacked the courage. He sobbed in silence. He spent the entire night wide awake, counting the ceiling fans, the leaks, the holes in the roof; he closed his eyes, tried to calm himself, all in vain. That was when, suddenly, a message popped into his head, clear in its meaning. A sentence. The beginning of what he wished to say to Lineu.

Restless, he waited for the day when the teacher came to the prison, he was afraid to miss his chance. He quickly sat down and delivered himself of the line. *One moment was all it took*, he wrote. He paused. He read it and then read it again. He continued. *Blow, winds, I howled amid the storm, notwithstanding the hoarseness that had dogged me since opening night*. The tragedy of Lear. His own. His hate for Stein, his laughing attack, the critics, the scorn for Lineu's lamentations in the dressing room. He was honest. He kept going, like a machine, writing in smaller and smaller letters so as not to run out of space. Directed back to his cell for roll call, he sat for a while before getting up. In a first, he expressed his irritation with the guard and was warned by the Pastor. His old shortness of breath assailed him once again that humid night. He was filled with anguish, he walked along the corridor between the beds, gave Greta the cold shoulder, and never again watched television.

He asked his aunt for paper, lots of it, reams, if possible. And pencils. Paper and pencil, plus cigarettes. He quit the sleeping pills, he wanted to stay alert. She obeyed without knowing whether to be happy or sad at his transformation. *I think he's worse*, Carine said on the subway heading home.

Sharp objects weren't permitted in prison. Pencils and pens included. Mario had to show restraint. He spent several hours planning out what he'd write. He was no longer addressing Lineu but himself. He complained about the idle hours, he wanted to write. He screamed through the bars about his right to free expression. The Pastor told him to quit his fussing and promised to help in return for a favor. *I give you my word as a man*, he said, sealing their pact. At night, when he dug out the cell phone from the wall and got the pack together, he sent for Lot. Mario took cautious steps forward, escorted by Greta. The band of criminals dialed a number and one of them, a young boy, his leg eaten up by erysipelas, set to moaning in a fake kidnapping. The other end of the line hung up. The boy lacked talent. The Pastor repeated the operation and delivered the device to Mario. It had been ages since he'd acted, he felt a flood of emotion. Dedicated to his task, he feigned terror, they shouldn't lose time bargaining, his life was on the line. He shed real tears. The terms of ransom negotiated, the Pastor hung up

211

satisfied. Mario earned the right to spend afternoons at school, working second shift on the telephone in the midnight farce.

He delivered what he'd written to his aunt. Ten months of dedication. She understood her task. On the envelope, the name Lineu Castro, composed in a neat, slanted hand. Neusa went to the studio, waited at the door until the actor showed his face, but Abraham had been killed off in the series long ago. An irritated Mario demanded she try harder, she asked him to be patient, she didn't know how to find the man in question. It was Carine who came upon Lineu by chance, in an ad for a play during a commercial break in the morning programming. He was onstage downtown, in *The Day They Kidnapped the Pope*. Mother and daughter bought tickets and went to the Teatro Ginástico one Saturday night to watch the João Bethencourt comedy. They laughed out loud at the Jewish taxi driver who takes the holy father home, then waited for the cast to filter out. Hearing the name Mario Cardoso, Lineu furrowed his brow. He wanted to flee, but took pity on the old lady. The imbroglio had brought him serious problems. The investigations had led the police to the accounts for Lear, they'd discovered the payoff scheme, which had contributed to Mario's conviction. Milena and Mota were indicted and the actors named in the case. Paulo, the heartthrob who had slugged Mario back at the hotel, made slanderous statements to the press, he had no doubt Gomes had been pushed. Lineu hadn't, either. He spent money he didn't have on a lawyer to guide him through his testimony, and he had awful recollections of the catastrophe. He wanted to stay far away but, a good heart, he couldn't ignore

Neusa's lament. She delivered the package, Lineu glanced at it silently and promised to read it, even against his will. He fulfilled his promise that same night. He arrived home late, made some coffee, sat at the table, and patiently opened the first of one hundred and seventeen pages numbered by hand in the right corner. Mario reminisced about their closeness in the dressing room, the envy he'd felt toward Arlindo and the laughing attack that seized him during *Lear*. It was all rather straightforward up until Paulo's cock-a-doodle-doo and the diapers. Suddenly, however, in a clean layout like the cover of a book, the narrative was interrupted by the title:

KING LEAR
By Mario Cardoso

With a shiver, Lineu continued reading. There were no more recollections, no through line. Mario had rewritten the play from start to finish, the way he'd remembered it. Act 1, Scene 1, the monarch divides his kingdom between his daughters; Act 1, Scene 2, Edmundo conspires against his brother Edgar; Act 2, Act 3, 4. . . . The King's lines, a few of the dialogues, especially those between Lear and the Fool, revealed a talent very nearly as precise as that of the original. What was more, Mario had written an imitation of the drama, relating, at times, the subtext that came to his mind during the spectacle; at others, the harshness of the critics. When commenting on certain scenes, he scornfully detailed Stein's staging, drawing tiny caricatures, like that of Paulo in diapers, to illustrate the costumes. And, what Lineu found even more unusual, random scribbles across the page, familiar names, Raquel, Guria, Milena, Marta, Bento, at first as footnotes and, toward the end, in place of the characters. Lear was the first to disappear, giving way to Mario. Gloucester, during the scene before the abyss, was transformed into Lineu; Amélia and Raquel took turns in Cordelia's skin; Regan became Milena; Marta, Goneril; Kent, Guria; and the Fool, Gomes. Gomes. The victim's mention made the old actor's heart go cold.

In a postscript, a favor. A favor. How could he deny it?

†

Lineu waited in the courtyard, surrounded by the families of the imprisoned. He had arranged the visit with Neusa, and Mario's aunt had thought it best to leave them alone. At seeing him, Mario cautiously approached and apologized for the inconvenience. The fellow actor peered at him, searching for signs of some mental disturbance, but Mario appeared serene. They embraced. They didn't say much, they didn't make conversation, there was nothing to say. Lineu was carrying a book under his arm, a play. *Macbeth. This the one?* he asked. *Yes, that's it*, Mario affirmed, *what I should have done*, he said, *instead of* Lear. Before saying goodbye Lineu wanted to know what end he ought to give to the manuscript. *Burn it*, the prisoner responded, *you can burn it, I buried that idiot in it.*

Mario returned to his cell with *Macbeth* in his hands. He had all the time in the world. The hours knew not the meaning of anguish. This idle time was in his favor.

Greta became interested in the black book cover with the photo of a pale white actress with braids and a haunted gaze. Lady Macbeth. *Is it a ghost story?* she asked. *It could be*, said Mario, *it opens with three witches. Shut uuup!* Greta squealed.

Mario described the plot, later he added a brief overview of Shakespeare. He gave a brief summary of the most important plays and spoke of the English theater's offstage intrigues. He detailed the assassination of Marlowe, a stabbing, just like her stabbing of the army sergeant, her client. He added that the men played the female roles during the golden age of the Bard. *Shut up, shut up, shut uuup!* she squealed. Mario read the famous soliloquy to his companion.

> *Tomorrow, and tomorrow, and tomorrow,*
> *Creeps in this petty pace from day to day,*
> *To the last syllable of recorded time;*
> *And all our yesterdays have lighted fools*
> *The way to dusty death. Out, out, brief candle!*
> *Life's but a walking shadow, a poor player,*
> *That struts and frets his hour upon the stage,*
> *And then is heard no more: it is a tale*
> *Told by an idiot, full of sound and fury,*
> *Signifying nothing.*

Greta was astonished, though she hadn't really understood. Mario repeated the stanza. He proposed they read the second scene of Act 2 together, in which Macbeth returns to the couple's bedroom after killing the king. Greta could barely make

215

out the syllables, but Mario persisted. *Listen silently to the words before letting them go*. He was going to carry on but gave up. That was what Guria had taught him, when he was still an aspiring actor. *Only in theater will you be free, Mario*, the director's final piece of advice came back to him. They read the scene again and again, spending the whole day on the ritual until they reached an acceptable result. Greta loved the Lady with same intensity with which she reviled Macbeth. *I'm terrified by weak men*, she said.

The school was no longer useful to Mario's ends, the classroom meant as much to him as a soccer field. It was as he waited in the cafeteria line that he began to notice the church, located at the end of the jail, after a long row of cells. The concrete benches, arranged in a semicircle before a small platform raised three feet from the ground. The wooden cross behind it and the pulpit, arranged in the middle of the stage. The stage. He had lived there for more than two years and had never noticed it. That night, he suggested to the Pastor that Greta participate in the scheme. Lifelong hormone injections had left him with a fine voice. He could pass as a woman, Mario noted, which would make the con all the more effective. He offered to train her himself but, in exchange, asked the boss to convince the prison director to free up the church so that he could give classes.

He became a dedicated teacher. He taught the transvestite basic tenets of relaxation, breathing, classic exercises, like the sunflower. He invested in her affective memory, bringing to the surface the many traumas Greta carried in her soul.

He meticulously tackled the scene in which Lady Macbeth, descended into madness, tries to wash the imaginary blood from her hands. Greta revealed herself to be a diligent student, with a tendency toward melodrama, not to mention a goldmine for the cell-phone gang. The Pastor relieved Mario, under the condition that he take on one more student, Splinter, a scowling orphan who had thrown himself upon a defenseless old man and killed him. The child's voice had the sound of guaranteed profits. Mario's prestige in the little clan only grew.

One morning like all the others, the Pastor was preparing for his morning sermon when Mario noted a certain weariness in the man. It was something that he'd noticed for some time, his voice dragging and without its former luster, his choice of verses ever briefer, and he read them without interest, closing with a brisk Our Father. Once prayers were over, the Pastor went back to being who he was: a crook with a pedigree, convinced that God had turned his back on him. That day, Mario carefully approached the man, he didn't want to lose his chance, and suggested he trade the Bible for *Macbeth*. *I've really had my fill of this same old story*, the felon admitted. *Give me that shit*. Mario showed him Scene 3 of the fourth act, in which Malcolm, son to King Duncan, Macbeth's victim, tries to persuade Macduff to raise arms against the usurper. At ease with the Testament, the Pastor had no difficulty understanding what was written. And he identified with the passage in which Macduff confesses his despotic inclinations.

"I should cut off the nobles for their lands; desire his jewels and this other's house. And my more-having would be as a sauce to make me hunger more, that I should forge quarrels unjust against the good and loyal, destroying them for wealth."

That's tight! the Pastor exclaimed with a smile, *folks is gonna wail. Macduff is testing the heir's good intentions*, Mario explained, *he says the opposite of what he thinks.* The Pastor was familiar with such artifice, it was thanks to such tricks that he was still alive, but the other way around, keeping himself impure while feigning chastity. He decided to take a chance, what harm could come of it, he thought, happy to trade Canaan for barbarian lands. They read the scene to a stunned crowd. The majority didn't grasp it, but those who did understand launched into an Our Father. Mario marveled at the Pastor's command. All that had been missing in his Lear, the regal carriage, the command, the irreverence, all that he had struggled to reach, on all fours, on the rug inside the speech coach's office in Copacabana, oozed from the imposing figure of the criminal. *Rio is a medieval city*, he thought, *divided into petty fiefdoms. Rocinha, Maré, and Jacaré are no different than Leicester, Kent, and Cornwall. The relationship of betrayal and power, so crucial in Shakespeare, the kingdoms and dukedoms, the battles to the death came alive on the former drug trafficker's tongue.* In the army of coarse men inside that crowbar hotel, Mario caught a glimpse of a cast.

With the Pastor's permission, he took over the morning sermon. He singled out a few acts of the play and read each scene in sequence, one each day, as they had done with the verses. Without clarifying that it was Shakespeare, he pretended it was all from the Bible, introducing Macbeth as an ambitious warrior, a contemporary of David, Solomon, or another hero of Israel. The cell listened, rapt, to the three witches' prophecies, the main couple's deadly ambition, the scorpions in the assassin's mind and the mystery: no man born of woman can harm Macbeth! They went wild when it was revealed that Macduff had been torn from his mother's womb and when Birnam Wood advances on the castle.

†

Neusa had her doubts about the gradual change in her nephew, who now was always excited to see her. Mario would grab his cigarettes and hurry away, fire in his eyes, he never sat down. He said he was happy. *Go figure*, his aunt said to her daughter on the way back home. Carine agreed with her mother's suspicion that her cousin had lost it once and for all.

The most pious asked to be transferred from D-7, something rotten was going on there. The Pastor pulled some strings and swapped three choirboys for three voodoo priests, until then housed outside the evangelical sector. Mario wanted them to play the witches. The day they arrived, they were welcomed to the clapping of palms, which raised the troupe's morale. The head of security came to peek through the bars, alarmed at the pandemonium echoing throughout the cell-block. He would have let it all pass, had he not seen Mario in the middle of the cell, rolling around like the Lady of the Night, the other prisoners delirious around him. A diabolic celebration. The prison director decreed an end to their antics and issued the order to separate Mario from the commoners. He was left to rot in solitary. He got his fever under control, feigned remorse, played the docile convict so he could return to D-7. He agreed to take over the morning Bible session from the Pastor and took on extra chores, in the cell, until he regained the guards' trust. He thought it prudent to keep Macbeth under wraps, rehearsing at night, with the cast from the cell-phone gang. The practice helped to give deeper meaning to the lines, like table readings, where, free from having to move around the space, the actors focus on the text. The theater classes at the church remained suspended for months, until the Pastor managed to get them reapproved. D-7 had returned to its former peacefulness and there was no further need for reprimand. When they once again stepped onto a stage, Mario was surprised at the troupe's performance, their nighttime work had taken effect, almost all of them were able to say their lines, and it was possible to give them marks. Faithful to Guria's teachings, Mario wrote out a spare staging, the actors arranged in a circle, on the floor, helping out with the sound effects for each scene while the characters took the center of the arena. It was already possible to glimpse the premiere.

During a routine visit to the prison by a human rights delegation, he saw his opportunity to dodge potential censorship. He took lead position against the bars, between variola and tuberculosis patients begging for help, and spoke of his ambition of producing Shakespeare with his fellow prisoners. A respectful Frenchwoman, head of the junta, who had the request translated, and then was given the inmates' history, fell in love with the successful actor lost amid that world of plagues. She asked to watch a rehearsal. Cornered, the director gave the order to bring out the cast. Mario, Greta, the voodoo priests, Splinter, the Pastor, and a handful more were escorted to the church. Mario took the cast by the hand, as he'd done in the days of *Hair*, and motivated their spirits with a tribal cry. The staging's local flavor, the witches and their spells, Greta's Lady, the Pastor's command, and Mario's undeniable talent thrilled Madame. She swore she would do what she could, congratulating Cleto, the prison director, for the initiative. The director, surprised at Mario's nerve, was confounded by the European woman's congratulations. The theater had its advantages, after all.

Cleto was a man with great experience in prisons: a former prison guard, he had come up the ranks and spent his life between prison walls. The difference was that he slept in his own bed; as for the rest, he suffered as much as the convicts did. He was poorly paid, was plagued by insomnia, had faced death threats, had been a hostage in more than one grisly rebellion, he'd seen many people kill and be killed. He knew that the prisoners were the ones who controlled the prison. Six guards for twenty-five hundred convicts? Not even if we tortured them, he was fond of saying. And all for what? Who gave a damn about him and the others there? The Frenchwoman's praise, the fact that she thought that the idea could have been his, inspired a rare feeling of pride, one he'd rarely felt in his post. Cleto became an ally. His brother worked at a samba school; he asked if they had some velvet left over, capes, or any outfits for a king or queen. He fetched what he could, a tin crown, some old instruments, and left them at the prisoners' disposal in a corner of the church.

On the appointed day, the human rights delegation showed up with a film crew. They wanted to record the experience for a documentary that would be shown at the UN. Mario lit up at the news. It had all begun with him, then with Greta, and later with the talent he'd sensed in the Pastor. He'd longed to return to the stage, but he never thought he would find himself, once again, before a camera. Before the shoot, they asked him to give a statement. Mario ran his fingers over the lens and felt the heat of the reflector, softening his wrinkles. He gave a bashful smile. Mario was back. When asked, he spoke of his innocence, he hadn't pushed anyone, though he felt as though he deserved to be there. *I think I killed myself*, he said, *I'm the one who died, and that's why I'm here*. He went over the process that had brought him to *Macbeth*, a detour of sorts, he concluded, a detour called *Lear*. *The theater is a dangerous line of work*. Mario spoke of his experience in the Pernambuco jungle and how much that had helped him with the prisoners; he recalled his professor, Campos, and his naive belief that we could make a new Cuba here at home, and regretted that he wasn't alive to see their work. He held forth about the notion of class hierarchy in Shakespeare that, in Brazil, paralleled the tension of the favelas; and he showered praise on Guria's *teatro essencial*. He praised Greta, her Diadorim in reverse, acknowledging that he owed his survival to her. Finally, he dedicated *Macbeth* to Raquel. *Raquel Jablonovski*, he said, *an actress who taught me that there's no difference between actor and character*.

The cameras were positioned in the church. Two on the sides of the nave and one in the middle. Before beginning, Mario gave a short speech to the audience of cleaners, prison guards, and the delegation. *It's impossible to capture the theater on film*, he claimed, *theater exists at the moment it is made, and afterward, it's over. Out out, brief candle.* . . . He thanked everyone for the opportunity, for their attendance, aware that only those present that afternoon, at that moment, would know, truly, what had passed there. Then he joined the circle of actors, a company formed by chance. He initiated the drumming of feet on the platform floor, the sound recalling Stein's storm. The Three Witches had announced the glory and the damnation of the Thane of Cawdor; and Mario—who knew all too well the character's weaknesses, ambition, and madness—fulfilled, as no actor had ever done before, his destiny as Macbeth.

ACKNOWLEDGMENTS

I would like to thank Ilda, Ilma, and all of Tijuca; my editors Emilio Fraia, Otávio Marques da Costa, and Luiz Schwarcz; Mario Sergio Conti and Flávio Moura; Evandro Mesquita, Elen Ignês, and Marcelo Freixo; the administration and inmates of Evaristo de Moraes Prison; and to the entire cast of *King Lear*, of which I was part.

ABOUT THE AUTHOR

FERNANDA TORRES was born in 1965 in Rio de Janeiro. The daughter of actors, she was raised backstage. Fernanda has built a successful career as an actress and has dedicated herself equally to film, theater, and TV since she was 13 years old. Over the last twenty years, she has started to write and collaborate on film scripts and adaptations for theater. She began to write regularly for newspapers and magazines in 2007 and established herself as a columnist. Her debut novel, *The End*, sold more than 200,000 copies in Brazil and was translated for publication in several countries including France, Italy, Spain, The Netherlands, Portugal, Hungary, and the United States. *Glory and its Litany of Horrors* is her second novel.

ABOUT THE TRANSLATOR

ERIC M. B. BECKER is a writer, literary translator, and editor of Words without Borders. He is the recipient of fellowships and residencies from the National Endowment for the Arts, the Fulbright Commission, and the Louis Armstrong House Museum. In 2014, he earned a PEN/Heim Translation Fund Grant for his translation of a collection of short stories from the Portuguese by Man Booker International Finalist Mia

Couto (Biblioasis, 2019). He has also published translations of numerous writers from Brazil, Portugal, and Lusophone Africa, including, Noemi Jaffe, Elvira Vigna, Paulo Scott, Martha Batalha, Paulo Coelho, and Carlos Drummond de Andrade. His work has appeared in the *New York Times*, Literary Hub, *Freeman's*, and Electric Literature's Recommended Reading, among other publications.